MURDER IN MANUSCRIPT

The murder of a mysterious recluse in
Barnet supplies Mr. Budd with one of
the most difficult cases of his career.
What is the connection between
Jonathan Haines, the murdered man,
and the typist who is found murdered
later that same day? Mr. Budd, with
the assistance of crime reporter Bob
Hopkins and the melancholy Sergeant
Leek, succeeds in piecing together all
the fragments of the puzzle — but not
until the stout superintendent has
suffered the most terrifying experience
of his life . . .

GERALD VERNER

---◆---

MURDER IN MANUSCRIPT

Complete and Unabridged

LINFORD
Leicester

First published in Great Britain in 1963

First Linford Edition
published 2013

A catalogue record for this book is available
from the British Library.

ISBN 978–1–4448–1763–8

Published by
F. A. Thorpe (Publishing)
Anstey, Leicestershire

Set by Words & Graphics Ltd.
Anstey, Leicestershire
Printed and bound in Great Britain by
T. J. International Ltd., Padstow, Cornwall

This book is printed on acid-free paper

1

The ticking of the small clock on the big desk was the only sound that broke the silence of the room. In that utter stillness it sounded loud and persistent, like repeated blows from a tiny hammer, filling the room with a relentless undercurrent that went on and on and on . . .

It was a large room, comfortable, even luxuriant. There were many deep-seated chairs of soft brown hide that blended with the russet hue of the heavy, velvet curtains that were drawn across the long French windows, and the rust colour of the thick pile carpet that covered the floor from wall to wall.

Dwarf bookshelves surrounded the oyster painted walls, filled with books of all kinds and shapes and sizes, their bright bindings lending a touch of brilliant colour to the rather sombre room, and throwing into relief the few ebony framed etchings that hung above them.

The massive desk of black, polished oak, on which the clock ticked so monotonously, stood near the window, its flat top littered with books and papers. Nearby was a table on which, within easy reach, was a tape-recorder.

In the wide hearth an electric fire threw out a warm and cheerful glow and was helped by the red-shaded lamp on the big desk to supply an air of warmth and cosiness to the apartment. The whole atmosphere was opulent. This was the study of a wealthy man, to judge from the appointments, for everything was expensive and of the best. But the man who sat in the padded chair at the desk did not harmonize with his surroundings. He was an odd figure with patchy, untidy hair that detracted from the high forehead, criss-crossed with lines, and would have looked more at home in a less pretentious place than this tastefully furnished room in which he sat, one long, thin hand playing nervously with a pencil, his deep eyes staring into vacancy.

It would have been impossible to guess at his age, though one might have put it in the late sixties from the heavily graven lines on the lean face and the almost complete whiteness of his patchy hair. In this guess as to the age of the man in the padded chair, the guesser would have been many years out.

Jonathan Haines was barely fifty. The attributes of age that seared his face and whitened his hair were attributable to a portion of his life that had destroyed his youth and warped his soul. Within the frail body, wrapped in an expensive, quilted silk, dressing-gown, there burned an anger that had grown stronger and stronger as the years went by until it had become a consuming passion — a passion to destroy the man who had been solely responsible for the ruin of his life.

And the hour that he had planned and schemed for was close at hand. The scheme was complete. Nothing, or so he hoped, could stop the suspended sword from falling on the head of his enemy.

A smile, grim and cruel, curved the hard, thin-lipped mouth, a smile in which no vestige of mirth brought warmth to the set face, as he pictured, as he had so often pictured, the final result of the past six months' untiring work. The blow would fall like a bolt from Heaven. His enemy was quite unprepared for the Nemesis that would overtake him.

That was the joke of it. That was the joy of the plan over which he had taken such elaborate precautions. It would burst upon the unsuspecting man like the sudden explosion of a bomb. He, Haines, would be miles away when the devastating effects of his labours reached their culmination, content in the knowledge that he had exacted full payment for those years of misery that lay behind.

The clock ticked on, its tiny hands drawing nearer and nearer to midnight, but the man at the desk sat immovable, oblivious of the passing of time, his whole mind exulting in the imaginative conception of his vengeance.

Outside, in the falling rain, the figure in the shiny raincoat, pressed his shivering body closer to the window as he peered in through a narrow slit in the curtains where they had been imperfectly drawn. Half-standing, half-crouching, he looked like some monstrous, evil nightbird. Muffling his face, so that only his eyes were visible, was a silk scarf, and upon his head he had drawn down the brim of a soft hat. Motionless, so still that he might have been carved out of stone, he crouched outside the window and watched and waited.

Half an hour passed slowly. The light from the room, percolating dimly through the chink in the curtains, was reflected in the eyes of the watcher. But he never moved.

Presently Jonathan Haines stirred. He rose to his feet with a sigh and stretched himself. It was getting late and he was weary. It was a weariness of soul rather than of body, a weariness that as long as life remained would never leave him. He switched off the electric fire. With his lean hands gripping the mantelshelf, he stood for a moment staring long and earnestly at a photograph in a silver frame that stood there and the hard expression on his face softened slightly. After a moment, suddenly, almost sharply, he turned away, walked to the door, snapped off the lights, and went out.

The light shining through the interstice in the curtains vanished and the eyes of the watcher vanished too. But still he waited. He was breathing, now, a little faster. Not a sound broke the stillness of the night except the gentle hiss of the falling rain and the faint sound of a car in the distance. Slowly the minutes dragged by. The man he had been watching had presumably gone to bed but the watcher could not afford to take risks. There was too much at stake. He had to be sure.

With infinite patience he waited. He was cold and wet. The rain had increased. From a thin drizzle it had developed into a steady downpour. But the man outside the window stuck to his post. He dared not give up. His liberty, his very life, depended on the successful silencing of the man who had so recently occupied that room.

He allowed an hour to drag slowly by, and then, as everything remained dark and silent within the house, he straightened up, took something from the pocket of his raincoat, and worked swiftly on the latch of the window. After a moment or two there was a slight crack and he felt the window give under his pressing fingers. The next second he was in the room. A wave of warmth greeted him but it was very dark — so dark that he paused just inside the window in case he should stumble over something and give warning of his presence. Gently he reclosed the window and stood listening. There was no sound except the ticking of the clock which seemed to his straining ears like the echoing thuds of his heart. Presently he drew a torch from his pocket and flashed the light about the empty room. He moved forward a pace, gave a swift glance round, and stopped to listen again.

The previous occupant of this room should be sleeping now somewhere in the house above. He would have to move carefully so as not to waken him. It would be easier to kill a sleeping man . . .

That was the first thing that had to be done. After, there would be time to search for the thing he must find and destroy . . .

The floor creaked slightly under his

weight as he moved toward the door. His hand was reaching for the knob when he stiffened suddenly and his muscles went rigid.

What was that?

He snapped out the torch and pressed himself against the wall behind the door. Was it his imagination or had there come to his straining ears the faint sound of movement beyond the closed door?

He listened intently but if there had ever been any sound it was gone now. Silence — silence so oppressive that to his heightened senses it seemed to possess a noise of its own and to throb and pound and palpitate until his ears rang with it . . .

There it was again!

A slight, almost inaudible sound — the sound of slippered feet!

He hugged the wall at the side of the closed door. The soft sound was unmistakable now — the approach of someone from the hall beyond the door.

The man, flattened against the wall, slipped the torch back into his pocket and withdrew a thin knife from which he slid the sheath. Almost holding his breath he waited.

The footsteps came nearer and stopped. There was a faint rattle of the handle as it was turned, the door was pushed open, and with a sharp click from the switch the room suddenly became flooded with light.

Motionless, the man behind the door watched as Jonathan Haines, still clad in his dressing-gown, came into the room. He paused with the partly open door in his hand and then advanced further. The man flattened against the wall sprang forward, the knife raised. Haines gave a quick exclamation and swung round in alarm, but he was too late!

The knife flashed down, gleaming in the light, and buried itself in the thin chest. Haines uttered a gasping sound and staggered. The knife, quickly withdrawn, struck again and yet again. Jonathan Haines crumpled, fell like a lay figure to the floor, clawed for a second with clutching fingers at the thick pile of the carpet, and lay still.

The murderer, breathing quickly,

stooped over the man on the floor to assure himself that he was dead. He was trembling violently, and under the scarf his face was wet and clammy. On the desk was a tray with a bottle of John Haig and some glasses. Clumsily, with his gloved hands, the murderer poured himself out a stiff whisky and swallowed it quickly. The spirit steadied his nerves. There was much he still had to do . . .

The clock ticked on but, now, there was no one to hear it. The sky lightened in the east and a pale sun rose, streaking the sky with golden fingers. Its light could not penetrate the darkness of the curtained room nor touch with warmth the cold body of the man who lay so still upon the thick pile of the rust-coloured carpet, a widening stain, of almost the same hue, spreading beneath him.

2

Mr. Budd came out of his cheerless office in Scotland Yard and moved slowly down the corridor on his way to the Assistant Commissioner's room. He moved without hurry, a large and majestic figure whose bulk almost filled the narrow passage. His heavy face was more than usually expressionless and his sleepy-looking eyes were half-closed under drooping lids.

This deceptively bovine outward appearance masked one of the keenest brains in the C.I.D. as many a complacent criminal had discovered when it was too late. Fat, lazy, Mr. Budd could summon up a wealth of unexpected energy when circumstances made it necessary.

Ponderously he arrived at last outside the door of Colonel Blair's office, raised a podgy hand, and knocked.

In answer to the muffled request from within, Mr. Budd opened the door and entered the office.

The Assistant Commissioner of the C.I.D., dapper and meticulously dressed as usual, looked over the broad flat-top desk.

'Sit down, superintendent,' he greeted.

The big man lumbered over to a chair in front of the desk and gingerly lowered his bulk into it.

'Well, sir?' he inquired.

Colonel Blair passed a hand lightly over his immaculate grey head.

'There's been a murder — at Barnet,' he said after a short pause. 'A man named Jonathan Haines. He was stabbed to death in the study of his house during the small hours of this morning. The local police have decided that the case is too big for them to handle and have asked for assistance.'

Mr. Budd fingered his cascade of chins.

'I see, sir,' he remarked. 'Did they supply any details?'

The Assistant Commissioner nodded. He picked up a sheet of notes torn from a pad and glanced at it.

'It seems rather an extraordinary affair,'

he remarked. 'That's why I'm putting it in your hands, Superintendent. You're particularly efficient with cases that are out of the ordinary.'

Mr. Budd considered this with mixed feelings. He wasn't at all sure that it was an enviable reputation to have. It meant that all the difficult cases were pushed on to him. He said, in a voice that was quite expressionless: 'What's so extraordinary about it, sir?'

'I haven't got all the details,' answered Colonel Blair. 'Detective Inspector Savage of the Barnet C.I.D. will fill you in. But the dead man seems to have been rather a queer sort of character. Hasn't been outside his house since he bought it three or four months ago. Robbery, or at least ordinary robbery, doesn't appear to have been the motive. The whole place was thoroughly ransacked but nothing of value seems to have been taken . . .'

Mr. Budd opened his sleepy-looking eyes very wide.

'How do the local police know that, sir?' he interrupted.

'There was a great deal of valuable

property left untouched,' answered the assistant commissioner. 'Silver plate and other stuff.'

'I don't think that proves anythin',' remarked Mr. Budd shaking his head ponderously. 'Might've been somethin' special that the murderer was after.'

'Very possibly you're right,' replied Colonel Blair. 'I've no doubt you'll get to the heart of it. You'd better go along to this place at Barnet — King's Lodge — as soon as possible. Everything is being left untouched until you arrive.'

'The local people've been pretty quick callin' in the Yard,' said Mr. Budd as he hoisted himself with difficulty to his feet.

'Yes, most commendable,' said Colonel Blair. He picked up a bulky folder and opened it. 'Good luck, superintendent.'

The big man made his way slowly and thoughtfully back to his office. Here was the beginning of another job of work which might prove easy or difficult. There was no telling until he had got all the details. It was very nice and complimentary of the A.C. to talk about 'cases that were out of the ordinary' but Mr. Budd was getting a little tired of that kind. He'd had quite a long spell of them lately. He thought that he'd prefer something a bit more easy for a change.

As he neared the door of his office, he stopped. A strange and completely unaccountable sound reached him from behind the closed door. It was a wierd and unholy wailing that sounded like a soul *in extremis*.

Mr. Budd turned the handle and flung open the door. The noise became even more nerve-racking now that it was no longer muffled.

'What's the matter?' demanded the big man, staring at the lean figure of Sergeant Leek from whom these awful sounds were eminating. 'Are you ill?'

The noise broke off sharply on the top of a high-pitched wail that would have been the envy of all the banshees in the wailing business. Leek, his mouth still open, but now mercifully silent, turned toward his superior with an injured expression.

'I didn't know you was there,' he said mournfully.

'What's the matter,' snapped the stout superintendent. 'Have you had a fit, or somethin'?'

'I was practisin',' explained Leek.

'Practisin',' repeated Mr. Budd in amazement. 'What for? A new type of air-raid warnin'?'

Leek's melancholy face assumed an expression of resignation.

'I was practisin' me pop number,' he answered.

'Your *what*?' demanded Mr. Budd.

'Me pop number,' said Leek. 'You've heard o' these pop singers, 'aven't you?'

A great and blinding illumination lit up Mr. Budd's brain. So this was the explanation for those excruciating sounds that had so startled him.

'You're not tellin' me that you're thinkin' of becomin' a pop singer, are you?' he inquired sarcastically.

'Yes, that's right,' answered Leek. 'It's all the rage these days. The teenagers swoon at 'em . . . '

'Heaven knows what they'd do at you,' interrupted Mr. Budd witheringly. 'Somethin' really horrible, I should think.'

'I'm a natural,' began the sergeant.

'You never spoke a truer word,' interrupted Mr. Budd, unkindly.

'There's lots an' lots o' money to be made at it,' Leek went on eagerly. 'If you get a recordin' in the top ten . . . '

'You won't get a record in the top ten or the bottom twenty,' snarled Mr. Budd. 'I s'pose this is another of your idiotic ideas — like hypnotism an' racin' and the football pools? You'd better give up wastin' your time an' get down to some honest work . . . '

'You oughter hear me sing 'Venus in Blue Jeans',' broke in the unabashed Leek. He flung back his head and opened his mouth. The expression on his lean face was so hideous that even Mr. Budd shied away.

'You stop it, d'you hear?' he interjected quickly. 'This is a respectable office, this is. I don't want to 'ear anythin' about 'Venus in Blue Jeans' or 'Mars in Red Pants' or 'Mercury in Bloomers'. We've got a job o' work to do so just get your mind off all this rubbish, will you, and pay attention.'

Leek's face slowly resumed its normal expression. He uttered a mournful sigh and shook his head sadly.

'One o' these days,' he said in a tone that was more in sorrow than in anger, 'you'll be payin' good money to 'ear me. When they put me on at the Palladium . . .'

'If they ever do I'll retire an' go an' live in Timbuktu,' snapped Mr. Budd. 'The only thing they'll ever put you on is the top of a barrel-organ in the Mile End Road. Now just you listen to me. There's been a murder in Barnet an' we're goin' along there at once. Get a car out front right away, will you, an' stop all this pop nonsense.'

With a sigh of resignation the unhappy sergeant picked up the house phone. A few seconds later they were in the police car *en route* for Barnet.

King's Lodge proved to be a fair-sized house near the common. It stood well back from the road in quite a little forest of trees. The short drive was moss-grown and neglected and so were the flower-beds and grass that flanked it. An atmosphere of gloom hung over the whole place as if it had put on mourning for its departed owner.

'Don't look a very cheerful spot, do it?' remarked Leek peering out the window of the car.

'We haven't come to a party,' retorted Mr. Budd.

The car drew up at the front door, and a constable on guard there came and opened the door.

'Inspector Savage is expecting you, sir,' he said, saluting smartly.

Mr. Budd squeezed himself out of the car and stepped gingerly on to the drive. At that moment a tall man with greying hair and a very rugged face, that looked as if it had been hewn out of wood with a blunt axe, appeared at the front door.

'Who's that?' he demanded in a parade-ground voice.

Mr. Budd introduced himself.

'Oh, good!' said Inspector Savage. 'Glad to see you. Come inside.'

The stout superintendent, followed by Leek, negotiated the shallow steps, and found himself in a spacious hall. If the outside of the house presented a neglected appearance, the same could certainly not be said of the interior. The hall was beautifully furnished and spotlessly clean. The wooden floor of polished oak was without a speck, the Persian rugs blended with the black oak and the silver fittings.

Judging from his surroundings, thought Mr. Budd as he looked around him sleepily, the dead man had been both well-off and a man of taste.

'This is a queer business,' remarked Inspector Savage. 'A very queer business. Don't mind admitting that it's out of my depth. I was just having a word with the dead man's housekeeper, Mrs. Bishop, when you arrived. P'raps you'd care to see her?'

Mr. Budd shook his head.

'Not for a moment,' he murmured. 'I'd like to get the hang o' the matter first. I don't know anythin' very much about it at present. I'm waitin' to get the details from you.'

'Yes, yes, of course. Understand,' said Savage. 'Better come in here, eh?'

He opened a door just inside the hall and ushered them into a small room that seemed to have been used for a cloakroom. There were, however, a small table and a chair and an oaken chest, apart from the row of pegs along one wall.

Mr. Budd ensconced himself on the chair and gave a prodigious yawn.

'Now, let's have it,' he remarked. 'Everythin' you know.'

Savage complied, and what he had to tell wasn't very much. The murder had been discovered by the housekeeper, Mrs. Bishop, and she had telephoned the Police station.

'Does she live in the house?' interjected Mr. Budd.

Savage shook his head.

'No. She used to come every morning at half-past seven, clean up and cook Haines's breakfast. She stayed until six-thirty at night, when he had his dinner, and then left for the night. There was a woman who used to come in during the day and help with the rough work.'

'I see,' murmured the big man.

'Haines'ud be alone in the house from six-thirty until this woman, Bishop, arrived on the followin' mornin'?'

The inspector agreed that this was correct.

'Unless he 'ad any visitors, friends or what-not?' said Mr. Budd.

'He never had any,' replied Savage. 'According to what Mrs. Bishop says, he never went out at all and nobody ever came to see him.'

'H'm, she was only here until six-thirty,' commented the stout superintendent. 'I don't see how she could know what happened after she left.' He rubbed gently at his cascade of chins. 'How did the murderer get in?' he asked after a slight pause.

'By forcing the catch of the French windows in the study,' answered Savage. 'They open into the garden.'

Mr. Budd got carefully to his feet and stretched himself.

'We may as well have a look at the study,' he said. 'I s'pose the photographs've been taken an' the finger-print chaps've done their stuff?'

Inspector Savage nodded.

'I've got the police surgeon's report too,' he said, in a tone that suggested that he didn't let the grass grow under *his* feet. 'The dead man was stabbed three times and any of the wounds would have been fatal.'

Mr. Budd made no comment to this. In fact, he looked as though he was on the verge of falling asleep. With his usual ponderous manner he followed Savage to the end of the hall and into the room where the crime had been committed. Just inside the door, the big man stopped and slowly looked round the comfortable apartment, taking in its arrangement. His half-closed eyes came to rest at last on the sprawling figure in the dressing-gown that lay face upward on the carpet.

'He hasn't been moved?' he murmured, going over and peering down at the dead man.

'No,' answered the inspector. 'I was very careful to see that nothing was disturbed.'

With a grunt, Mr. Budd lowered himself onto one knee. He looked at the

23

thin cuts in the front of the dressing-gown that corresponded with the knife stabs. They were close together and in the region of the heart.

'The knife hasn't been found, I s'pose?' asked Mr. Budd without looking up.

'No. I looked for it but the murderer must have taken it with him.'

'H'm! I wonder what else he took with him?' grunted Mr. Budd struggling to his feet. 'Let's have a look at this window.'

He lumbered over to the French window and examined the fastening. The brass latch was hanging loose; the screws wrenched from the woodwork. The white powder of the fingerprint man was everywhere.

'He used a jemmy, I should think,' muttered Mr. Budd. 'Not a professional, eh? Clumsy piece o' work.'

He pulled the window open and stepped gingerly outside. There was a gravel path, broad and rather wet, that ran across the entire back of the house.

Mr. Budd looked at it with a ruminating eye.

'There should be traces here of our

24

man,' he remarked. He leaned forward and peered at the soggy surface.

'I've already examined the place for footprints,' volunteered Savage.

'So I see!' retorted the big man dryly, and the inspector looked a little sheepish.

'I'm afraid my men *did* walk over it a bit,' he apologized, but Mr. Budd wasn't listening. From the gravel path a fairly large plot of ragged, unkempt grass stretched away to a belt of evergreen shrubbery. Beyond, rose a small clump of trees.

The stout superintendent eyed this for a moment and then lowered his eyes to the rank expanse of grass. There was some kind of track visible where the long grass had been bent down.

The mournful Leek was standing in the window staring at the trees. There was a vacant look in his eyes and his thin lips were moving gently. Only the faintest of faint sounds issued from his mouth but the keen ears of Mr. Budd detected them.

'She's Venus in blue . . . '

'Come here,' snapped the stout superintendent, swinging round on his subordinate.

'I'm goin' over to them trees. I want you to come with me.'

Reluctantly the lean sergeant shambled to his side.

'What are we goin' there for?' he demanded.

'Because I believe that the murderer came that way,' said Mr. Budd, 'an' there may be more an' better traces of him than this path which has been trampled over by a herd of elephants.'

'Why do you want me?' inquired Leek.

'I'll admit that anybody wanting you for anything must seem strange,' retorted Mr. Budd witheringly. 'But, in case you may have forgotten it in your zeal to shine as a pop singer, it happens to be the job for which you draw your pay. Though why you draw it is somethin' that nobody has yet been able to fathom. Maybe the powers that be feel benevolent towards you.'

'I know my job,' said Leek complacently.

'You keep your knowledge to yourself,' said his superior. 'Come along, an' forget Venus for a bit, will you?'

He set off along the grass track with Leek trailing along in his rear. Inspector Savage stood hesitating on the gravel path. He had not been asked to join Mr. Budd and wondered what he should do. Eventually, he decided to follow.

They came to the shrubbery and saw that backing it was a wooden fence that separated the garden of King's Lodge from what appeared to be a small copse.

In the wet earth of the shrubbery they saw the clear impression of a pair of thick boots going towards the fence.

Mr. Budd paused and peered at them closely.

'H'm,' he muttered almost to himself. 'Interestin' an peculiar.'

'What is?' asked Savage who had caught up with them.

'These prints,' replied the big man. 'They give us a bit of information about this feller.'

Inspector Savage looked down at the prints, and his brow puckered.

'I don't see what you mean,' he said.

'Maybe you don't,' answered Mr. Budd, 'but you will.'

Keeping well clear of the line of footprints, the big man followed them to the dividing fence. Close to it the prints were confused and overlapping. Near at hand, in the soft earth, was the impression of a hand, the fingers wide spread.

'Looks as if our friend had a fall,' said Mr. Budd. 'He slipped gettin' over the fence an' put out his hand to save himself. H'm. What's on the other side?'

Carefully avoiding the impression in the soft earth, he peered over the low fence. The belt of trees was quite a narrow one and ran down a sloping bank to another fence of barbed wire. Beyond this was a footpath running along the edge of the common.

'Not much good tryin' to trace the prints any further,' grunted the big man. 'We'll be gettin' back to the house. I want casts made o' these,' he pointed to the footprints and the impression of the hand. 'Can you arrange that?'

Inspector Savage nodded.

'I'll have it done at once,' he said.

'Good,' remarked Mr. Budd. 'Now, I'd

like to have a word with this woman, what's-her-name? — Bishop.'

Mrs. Bishop was sitting in the kitchen. She was a woman of uncertain age, as far as outward appearances went, for her hair was of the colour which is so often referred to by novelists and press agents as 'honey blonde' but by chemists as peroxide of hydrogen. Her mouth was large and the red of her lips owed nothing to nature. Her eyes were of a peculiar faded blue, as though the recent tears, traces of which could still be seen furrowing the make-up on her cheeks, had washed the dye out.

'Now m'am,' said Mr. Budd in his most avuncular manner. 'There're just one or two things I'd like you to tell me, if you don't mind.'

Mrs. Bishop sighed and dabbed at her eyes with a wisp of handkerchief.

'I feel so upset,' she said, shaking her head. 'So terribly upset. It was such a shock. This is the first situation of this kind that I've ever had, you see. I was hoping to get a position with some people in Bombay as a governess. That is my real occupation. But they engaged a black woman. Can you imagine it? *So* disappointing. What . . . ?'

'Yes, yes, it must have been,' broke in Mr. Budd. 'Now, I'm sure you'll realize, m'am, that we have a lot to do. I'd be glad if you'd just answer my questions as briefly as possible.'

Mrs. Bishop sniffed and transferred the handkerchief from her eyes to her nose. But she made no verbal reply.

'You were housekeeper to the dead man?' went on the stout superintendent.

'I suppose you would call it that,' she answered.

'How long had you been in his employ?'

'Nearly three months, perhaps a little longer. Yes, I think it was a *little* longer.'

'How did you obtain the situation?'

'I answered the advertisement in the local paper. I wasn't going to at first because it said that no woman under thirty need apply, but Mr. Haines must have liked my appearance because he engaged me at *once*.'

'Maybe all the make-up an' the rest of

it didn't deceive him,' said Mr. Budd, but he said it to himself. Aloud, he continued: 'Had you ever met Mr. Haines before?'

'Oh, no,' she replied quickly. 'That was the first time I ever saw him.'

'You didn't live in the house?' asked Mr. Budd.

Mrs. Bishop looked shocked.

'Dear me, of course not,' she answered. 'I could not possibly have done that. Mr. Haines was here entirely by himself — I mean, there were no other women here. What *would* people have thought . . . '

Mr. Budd wasn't interested.

'What time did you get here in the mornin' an' when did you leave at night?' he interrupted her.

'I used to get here about eight o'clock in the morning, get his breakfast and tidy up. Then I'd be here to see to his lunch. I prepared his dinner at half-past six and then I went home. Of course, there was a woman who used to come to do the *rough* work. I couldn't do *that*, naturally.'

'I see.' Mr. Budd nodded and pulled gently at his nose. 'What sort of man was Mr. Haines?'

'Well, I don't know very much about him . . . '

'Did you like him?'

'Yes, I liked him. I always thought he was most kind and considerate. Not like most men. He was a little eccentric but — yes — I liked him.'

'A bit eccentric, was he?' murmured Mr. Budd, giving his nose a rest and pulling his left ear. 'How was he eccentric, m'am?'

'Well,' she explained after a slight pause, 'he never went outside the house, not once all the time I've been here, and nobody ever came to see him. He used to spend all his time in the study writing . . . '

'Writing?' interposed Mr. Budd, opening his half-closed eyes. 'What was he writing?'

'I think it was a play . . . '

'Did he tell you so?'

Mrs. Bishop shook her golden head.

'No, he never told me what he was writing,' she said.

'Then how do you know it was a play?' demanded the stout man.

'Well,' she replied after a slight hesitation and with some confusion, 'I found a sheet of it once. Mr. Haines was always very particular to lock all his writing away, but this must have dropped under his desk without his noticing it. I found it when I was dusting the study one morning. He was very annoyed — quite *angry* about it.'

'Can you remember what it was about?'

'Only that it had something to do with a murder,' she answered.

Mr. Budd looked at Leek. The lean sergeant's lips were moving gently and his eyes were fixed on the corner of a kitchen cabinet. He was, Mr. Budd thought with exasperation, quite oblivious of what was going on.

'Did you hear that?' he demanded loudly.

Leek started. His mournful eyes turned toward his superior and his lean jaw dropped.

''Ear what?' he answered vaguely. 'I didn't hear anythin' . . . '

'I didn't think you did,' snarled Mr. Budd. 'Too busy with Venus, I s'pose.

You'd better pull yourself together, me lad. We're not doin' any poppin' at the moment. We're investigatin' a murder an' if you don't keep your mind on your job we'll be investigatin' another.'

'I'm sorry,' apologized the lean sergeant. 'I was just workin' out a gimmick . . . '

'Never mind your gimmicks,' snapped the big man crossly. 'Just you pay attention.'

Leek mumbled something under his breath and Mr. Budd turned to the rather surprised housekeeper.

'Now, m'am,' he said. 'You say this play that the dead man was writin' was somethin' to do with a murder? Can you remember any more about it?'

'No, I'm afraid I can't,' she confessed. 'I only remember seeing the word 'murder'.'

Mr. Budd frowned. Leek fidgeted with his feet and wondered what it was all about. It seemed to him to matter very little whether the dead man had been writing a play or a treatise on the domestic habits of beetles. He wasn't very interested in either case. What he had to

34

work out was what sort of style he should adopt as a pop singer. It would have to be something that would mark him out from all the others. That's what you wanted these days, a gimmick. He supposed, however, that he'd better pay attention to what was going on, otherwise there'd be trouble.

He sighed as Mr. Budd continued:

'You say that Mr. Haines never had any visitors,' went on the stout superintendent. 'But that was only durin' the time you was in the house. He might've had somebody call after you'd left, mightn't he?'

'He might,' she agreed, 'but I never found any traces of anyone having been.'

'Did you ever come back in the evening?'

'No, never.'

'How did he pay you? By cheque or by cash?'

'In cash.'

'Do you know if he had a bank account?'

She shook her head.

'I don't know. He used to give me the

money to pay the tradespeople. They were always paid weekly.'

'You did all the shopping that was required?'

'Yes, that was part of my duties.'

'What about letters?' Mr. Budd went on. 'Did he have many?'

'He never had any to my knowledge.'

Mr. Budd sighed. There was very little, at present, to go on. The dead man appeared to have no background nor any contacts. Until a great deal more could be learned about him it was not going to be easy to discover why he had been murdered and by whom.

'Is there anything at all, m'am,' he persisted, 'that you can recollect that might help us?'

Mrs. Bishop drew her brows together in a frown, but after a little while she shook her head.

'I'm afraid there's nothing,' she declared.

'Did you ever post anything for Mr. Haines,' urged Mr. Budd. 'Take a message anywhere?'

'I took a parcel to the post office about a week ago,' answered the woman. 'I'd forgotten that . . . '

'Come now,' broke in the stout superintendent. 'That's something. Who was it addressed to?'

'I don't remember,' she began and then: 'Wait, it was a registered parcel — quite a large one. I gave the receipt to Mr. Haines. No, I didn't,' she corrected hastily. 'I was going to, but something intervened . . . Now, what was it?'

'Never mind that,' said Mr. Budd. 'What did you do with the receipt?'

'It must be in my bag,' Mrs. Bishop reached out a hand for a large handbag that stood on the table. She opened it and searched in the interior. Presently, she produced a crumpled piece of paper.

'Here it is,' she said holding it out.

The big man almost snatched it from her fingers. Smoothing out the crumpled slip he peered at it. The pencilled inscription was so faint and worn that he could scarcely read it. He managed to do so at length, however, and read it aloud:

'*Miss Phyllida Loveridge, 166a, High Street, Barnet*'.

'Do you know who Miss Loveridge is, m'am?' he asked, but Mrs. Bishop could supply him with no information.

At that moment there came the sound of confused voices in the hall. The constable's voice was raised in protest, drowned by a younger voice that cried:

'I tell you I know Superintendent Budd,' it declared. 'We're as close as peas in a pod! He'll dance the can-can with joy when he knows I'm here . . .'

Mr. Budd uttered an exclamation. With surprising agility, he crossed the kitchen and opened the door. The next moment he was in the hall facing the flustered constable and a small, wiry little man with flaming red hair.

'What do you want, Hopkins?' demanded Mr. Budd, and the red-haired man swung round.

'Hello, hello,' he greeted. 'The great man himself — and when I say 'great' I don't mean in point of size . . .'

'I s'pose you're coverin' this murder for that wretched paper of yours?' grunted Mr. Budd.

'The man who's never wrong,' retorted

38

Bob Hopkins, known to his friends as 'Hoppy'. 'That's the situation in a nutshell. Come on, my dear old chum, tell me all about it.'

'I wish I could,' said Mr. Budd fervently.

'That's how it is, eh?' remarked Hoppy. 'Not to worry. Between us we will bust the case wide open.' He pulled out a packet of cigarettes, extracted one and put it in his mouth. 'What do you know so far?'

'Nothin' ' answered Mr. Budd shortly.

'We practically start from scratch, then,' said Hoppy lighting his cigarette and inhaling a huge lungful of smoke. 'Is the redoubtable Leek with you?'

Mr. Budd nodded gloomily.

'An' a fat lot o' good he's goin' to be,' he said. 'All he can think of is Venus an' blue jeans an' a lot of tripe about bein' a pop singer.'

Hoppy stared and then he went into a hoot of laughter.

'Leek a pop singer,' he exclaimed with difficulty. 'Oh, my suffering cats! Can you beat it?'

Mr. Budd frowned darkly.

'You can laugh,' he growled wrathfully, 'but it isn't funny. His 'ead's so full of all this pop muck that he's no use at all . . . '

'Then I've arrived in the nick of time,' said Hoppy quickly. 'I will be your crutch, your staff, your trusted Watson. Put me in the picture and we'll begin at once.'

Mr. Budd regarded him thoughtfully.

'That might not be such a bad idea,' he said.

3

Mrs. Bishop, receiving permission to depart after leaving her address, went gratefully away, leaving a pungent odour of cheap perfume behind her.

Mr. Budd, perched on the kitchen table, rapidly outlined the case, so far as he knew it, to Hoppy, while that energetic individual strode up and down smoking a succession of his own particular choice of cigarette. The lean sergeant rested his long back against a corner of the dresser and stared mournfully at the floor.

'And that,' ended the stout superintendent, 'is all that is known so far. If I let you in on it you've got to promise that you won't print a line unless I give you permission. Understand?'

'Have I ever?' protested Hoppy.

'I'll admit you're not as bad as some,' grunted Mr. Budd grudgingly. 'Now, I'm goin' to have a look at the study and take a general look-see round to make sure that nothin' important has been over-looked.' He surveyed the melancholy Leek. 'If you can stop imaginin' that you're the top ten pop singers all rolled into one,' he said sarcastically, 'p'raps you might join us.'

'I'm willing to do me duty,' answered Leek.

'If you did your duty you'd resign from the p'lice force,' snapped Mr. Budd. 'Come on, let's get busy. I want to go along an' see Miss Phyllida Loveridge as soon as possible.'

The body of the murdered man had been removed when they entered the study. With the assistance of Leek and Hoppy, the big man made a quick but systematic search of the big writing table. They found nothing there, however. Nor was there anything in the chaotic confusion on the floor, where the contents of the drawers had been strewn everywhere. While they were in the middle of their search, Inspector Savage came in.

'I've arranged for those plaster casts you wanted,' he said. 'They're taking them now.'

'Good,' said Mr. Budd. 'There don't seem to be anythin' here,' he added despondently. 'If there *was* anythin' that 'ud give us a clue to Haines's past or anythin' about him, the murderer must've taken it away.'

'Hello, hello!' exclaimed Hoppy suddenly. 'What's this?'

He had gone over to the mantelpiece and picked up a photograph that was lying face downward. It was the photograph of a girl, young, and more than ordinarily pretty. Her large eyes stared steadily out from beneath pencilled brows, her mouth was smiling . . .

'What on earth is this doing here?' ejaculated Hoppy in surprise.

'What d'you mean? Who is it?' demanded Mr. Budd, lumbering over to his side.

'You ought to know if you read your newspapers,' answered the reporter. 'It's Janice Sheridan, the actress. She's playing the leading part in the show at the Majestic Theatre.'

'Is she now?' remarked Mr. Budd thoughtfully. 'That's very interestin' an' peculiar. What's her picture doin' here, I wonder?'

Hoppy put the photograph down and shrugged his shoulders.

'Ask me another,' he said. 'Maybe Haines bought the thing.'

The big man looked far from satisfied with this suggestion.

'Maybe there's more in it than that,' he grunted. 'Maybe this woman, what's-her-name? — Sheridan — can give us some information. I'll have to go an' see her.'

He had been looking about the room while he spoke and, spotting the tape-recorder, moved over to it.

'This is rather funny,' he murmured. 'There're no reels of tape on this thing. Only one empty one. You couldn't use it.'

'I noticed that,' put in Inspector Savage.

Hoppy joined them.

'Perhaps he'd filled them up,' he said. 'He may have wanted to keep a permanent record of something . . . '

'See if you can find 'em anywhere,' said Mr. Budd. 'There should be some spares, surely.'

They searched everywhere but there was no sign of anything of the kind.

'Queer,' muttered Mr. Budd, rubbing his chins. 'Very queer. You'd think they'd be here somewhere, wouldn't you? Unless, of course, the murderer took 'em . . . '

'What for?' demanded Hoppy.

'That's what I'd like to know,' said the stout superintendent. 'H'm, very curious.'

He yawned.

'What do we do next?' inquired Hoppy.

'We pay a visit to this woman in the High Street,' said Mr. Budd. 'Miss Phyllida Loveridge . . . '

Savage uttered an exclamation.

'She's a typist,' he said. 'Got a combined flat and office in the High Street . . . '

'A typist, is she?' interrupted the big man. 'I ought to've guessed it.'

'Why?' asked Savage. 'How did you know anything about her?'

Mr. Budd repeated what the housekeeper had told him concerning the parcel.

'I'll bet that it contained this play she

thinks he was writin',' he said.

'There's no proof that he was writing a play,' objected Hoppy. 'She only *thought* that's what it was.'

'Well, we shall soon know one way or the other,' said Mr. Budd. 'Come on, there's nothin' much to learn here. I'd be glad, though inspector, if you'd have a look over the rest of the house just in case there's anythin'. I'll be back after I've seen this woman, Loveridge.'

They left the inspector in charge and made their way to the police car which was waiting outside the front entrance.

Mr. Budd gave his instructions to the driver and got heavily in, sinking back into a corner with a grunt of satisfaction. Leek and Hoppy followed him.

'You ought to be very grateful to me,' said Mr. Budd, taking out one of his black cigars and sniffing at it.

'I'm not going to be grateful if you're going to poison me with that thing,' declared Hoppy.

'These are good cigars,' said Mr. Budd. 'They've got a real flavour, I can tell you.'

'You don't have to — I've smelt 'em,'

said the reporter. 'Tar and old rope with a dash of rocket fuel . . . '

'You don't appreciate a good smoke, that's what's the matter with you,' remarked the big man. 'But you needn't worry. I'm not goin' to smoke it. I haven't got time to enjoy it. I'm just takin' an appreciative sniff.'

'Thank heaven for that!' said Hoppy fervently.

'I don't 'old with smokin', meself,' remarked Leek, shaking his thin head. 'It's bad for the vocal cords.'

'You don't have to worry about that if you're thinking of being a pop singer,' said Hoppy. 'The vocal cords don't count. None of the pop singers I've ever heard could sing a note properly.'

'That's why they write all these brashy songs,' agreed Mr. Budd. 'They couldn't sing a real song with any tune in it. It'ud beat 'em flat. 'Venus in blue jeans', 'Return to sender' an' all the other junk. The words are just a lot o' tripe an' the music, if you can call it that, is all alike. I never can tell the difference in any o' these so-called 'tunes'.'

'The teenagers like 'em,' said Leek. 'You hark at 'em.'

Mr. Budd grunted disgustedly.

'A whole lot of witless squeals,' he commented with withering scorn. 'You wouldn't think there was a brain among 'em. I'll tell you somethin'. A few years ago all your present-day pop singers, as you call 'em, would've been pelted off the stage with rotten cabbages.'

'You don't understand,' said Leek. 'They get worked up an' excited when they see their favourite or 'ear 'im on the radio.'

'They'd do better to get worked up over somethin' sensible,' growled the big man. 'All these wailin' asses, cryin' about some girl who's let 'em down. Crawlin' about at her feet like a lot o' spineless maggots. An' the girls are just as bad. None of 'em have got a penn'orth of guts among the lot of 'em. You can't tell me that the people who write the stuff have got any intelligence, either. Stringin' a lot o' words together that don't mean anythin'.'

'The whole thing boils down to sex,'

said Hoppy, lighting one of his eternal Woodbines. 'After all, the main theme of any song, ballad, or what-ever-you like, has been love.'

'You can degrade anythin',' said Mr. Budd.

The police car pulled up at that moment, and the stout superintendent peered out the window.

'Here we are,' he announced unnecessarily, and hoisted himself out of the seat.

166a proved to be a shop and, judging from the window display, sold television sets, tape-recorders, radios, and gramophone records. The door was set on a slant in an alcove, and beside it, almost at right angles, was a second door, open, which disclosed a narrow flight of linoleum-covered stairs leading upwards. On the side of this second door were several cards over corresponding bell-pushes. On one of these, neatly typed in capital letters, was the inscription: '*Phyllida Loveridge. Typewriting Bureau. 1st. Floor.*'

Mr. Budd rang the bell and waited. Nothing happened and he rang again.

Still nothing happened. Nobody took the slightest notice.

'Let's go up?' suggested Hoppy.

Mr. Budd eyed the stairs doubtfully. They were very narrow for a man of his bulk, but there was certainly a lot of sense in the reporter's suggestion. With a grunt of agreement, he slowly mounted the stairs to the first floor. There was only one door on the small landing but it bore above the letter-box another card similar to the one downstairs except for the addition of the word 'office'. The door was shut and appeared to be locked. The big man searched for a bellpush. There wasn't one, and he thumped on the door with his clenched fist.

Hoppy had gone up the remaining stairs to explore the regions above and called down.

'I think she lives up here,' he said.

'More stairs,' growled Mr. Budd, but he went up and joined the reporter on the second floor, followed by Leek.

Here there was another door which also bore a type-written card but with the word 'private' instead of 'office'.

'Let's hope the woman's at home,' grunted Mr. Budd. There was a brass knocker in the centre of the door and he gave a heavy rat-tat-tat.

'She must be out,' said the lean sergeant when nothing more happened than had happened downstairs.

It was Hoppy's sudden exclamation that drew the stout superintendent's attention to something on the shabby linoleum that covered the landing. It showed a reddish streak along the bottom of the door, staining the floor.

Mr. Budd's heavy face changed. His eyes became suddenly alert.

'That's blood!' he ejaculated. 'There's somethin' wrong here!'

Without wasting further breath he hurled himself against the closed door. It resisted at first but it had never been made to withstand such a battering ram. The screws holding the lock tore out of the old wood, and the door crashed back against the wall of a narrow passage within. The place was gloomy, but Hoppy found a switch in the wall near the door and pressed it down.

A pendant bulb in the ceiling glowed into life, and they stared in horrified surprise at what they saw.

The small and narrow hall was in chaotic disorder. Two chairs that normally must have stood against the wall were overturned. A long rug had been kicked into an untidy heap. In the midst of this chaos, face downwards in a puddle of partly dried blood, lay the body of a woman.

4

Mr. Budd stood stock-still in the open doorway and stared down at this unexpected spectacle.

'Don't move, either of you,' he warned, and very cautiously advanced further into the little hall, careful to avoid treading on the polished linoleum more than he could help. Stooping, he pulled the rumpled carpet nearer to him and knelt down beside the motionless woman.

'Go an' get on to the p'lice station,' he said to Leek. 'Tell 'em to get the doctor over here as soon as possible. Get hold of Inspector Savage as well.'

Leek nodded and stumbled away down the stairs.

'Is she dead?' asked Hoppy. He was fairly well hardened to unpleasant sights but his face looked a little pale.

'I shouldn't think there was any doubt about that,' answered Mr. Budd. He pointed to the handle of the knife that protruded from the woman's back. 'We can't move her until the doctor's seen her.'

'This is horrible,' muttered the reporter. 'I suppose she was killed by the same person who killed Haines?'

'Yes, I should say that was pretty well certain,' agreed the big man. He got up and looked about him.

'Why? What's at the bottom of it?' demanded Hoppy.

Mr. Budd shrugged his massive shoulders.

'Now, you're askin' me somethin' I can't tell you,' he said. 'We'll be in a better position to answer that when we've had a look round. We'd better not do anythin' until after the doctor's done his stuff an' the photographer an' fingerprint chaps have done theirs.'

He went out on to the little landing and peered down the stairs.

'The people in the shop wouldn't have heard anythin',' he remarked almost to himself. 'They'd have been gone, I should think. Obviously, they can't live on the premises. The woman had all the top part, apparently.'

'I suppose, she *is* Phyllida Loveridge?' said Hoppy.

'We'll soon know that, too,' said Mr. Budd. 'Meanwhile all we can do is wait.'

They hadn't very long to wait. Leek re-appeared followed by a small, wiry, dark haired man who introduced himself as Doctor Collis, the police surgeon. Behind him came Inspector Savage and two other men.

The stout superintendent briefly explained, and the doctor made his examination. The woman was quite dead and had been dead for some hours. The knife had entered the heart and she had died almost instantly. Inspector Savage definitely identified her as Phyllida Loveridge, whom he had known slightly. The photographer took several pictures of the position of the body and the fingerprint man was told to 'do his stuff'.

'Now, we can have a look at the rest of the place,' said Mr. Budd.

There were two rooms opening off the narrow hall, one on either side. At the end of the hall was a curtained window. This was shut and the catch had not been tampered with. The first door, the one on the left, led to a comfortably furnished sitting-room. A square of grey carpet occupied the centre and, drawn up to a gas fire that was out, were two easy chairs. A book, half-open, rested on the arm of one of them. In the middle of the carpet was an oval table containing a bowl of flowers and the remains of a meal on a tray. A settee by the window and a small book-case with several books completed the furnishings.

It had been a very tidy room, probably, at one time. Now, it looked as if an avalanche had struck it!

The bureau part of the bookcase had been forced open and its contents littered the floor. The cushions had been pulled from the settee and flung down in a crumpled heap. Everything that could be moved had been moved. The room had been thoroughly searched.

'Just like the study at King's Lodge,' murmured Mr. Budd, looking round the room with narrowed eyes. 'Our murderer was lookin' for somethin' here, too.'

'What could he have been looking for?' asked Savage.

'I've got a vague notion about that,' grunted Mr. Budd. 'I'm not goin' to say what I think at the moment. I might be wrong an' I wouldn't like that.'

Inspector Savage looked as if he rather doubted this, but he said nothing.

Mr. Budd knew quite well what the inspector was thinking. It was one of his peculiarities, which all his friends found extremely exasperating, that he insisted on keeping his ideas to himself until he had proved them, to his own satisfaction, to be right. He began to probe and peer about among the littered papers on the floor. Suddenly he picked up a single sheet and gave a grunt of satisfaction.

'What have you found?' inquired Hoppy quickly.

'A very interestin' thing,' replied Mr. Budd. 'It's a bill.'

'A bill?' asked Savage.

'Made out to Haines,' said the big man. 'Mrs. Bishop was right about his writin' a play.'

Hoppy peered over the stout man's

shoulder. The paper he held in his chubby hand was a neatly typed account. It was addressed to Jonathan Haines, Esq., King's Lodge, Barnet, and was for the typing of two copies of a three-act play entitled 'The Crime'. It included the postage for sending one copy to Guy Maitland, Esq., 6 Mount Street, London, W.1.

Hoppy whistled.

'Guy Maitland,' he repeated.

'You know who he is?' asked Mr. Budd quickly.

'Most people do,' replied the reporter. 'He's a well-known theatrical producer . . . '

'A theatrical producer, is he?' murmured Mr. Budd. 'Now, that's very interestin' an' peculiar.'

'I get you,' exclaimed Hoppy suddenly. 'That picture — on Haines's mantelpiece . . . '

'A well-known actress an' a well-known producer,' broke in the stout superintendent, 'an' a feller who had written a play. There you are, you see. All connects up, don't it?'

'More than you think,' cried Hoppy

excitedly. 'Guy Maitland was a man who first brought Janice Sheridan from playing in provincial repertory companies and put her in the West End of London.'

'What's all this got to do with the murder?' asked Inspector Savage with a puzzled frown.

'Maybe nothin' — maybe a lot,' said Mr. Budd. 'It's just one o' those things that're worth thinkin' about.' He rubbed gently at his fat chin. 'This bill mentions *two* copies of this play,' he remarked thoughtfully. 'I'd like to know what's happened to the other one.'

'I should think the most likely place would be in the office downstairs,' said Hoppy.

'I should be glad to believe you,' answered the stout superintendent, frowning. 'There ought to be some keys here somewhere. Has that feller finished?'

The fingerprint man looked round.

'Yes, I've finished,' he said. 'Nothing much, though. The chap who did this wore gloves.'

'I'd've been surprised if he hadn't,' remarked Mr. Budd. He went over to where the dead woman's handbag lay among the debris on the floor. Picking it up, he peered inside.

'No keys here,' he grunted. 'See if you can find 'em, will you? I don't think you will, but you can try.'

They made a careful search of the small flat but there were no keys to be found.

'We'll have to break open the door,' said Mr. Budd wearily. 'He must've come here first, killed the woman, taken the keys and then gone down to the office. I expect he left the keys inside.'

'What for?' asked Inspector Savage.

'Because he was lookin' for somethin',' said the big man. 'The same thing he was lookin' for at Haines's place. Come on, let's take a look at that office.'

As they came down the stairs a man appeared at the foot. He was a middle-aged, respectable-looking man, who eyed them suspiciously.

'What's going on up there?' he demanded.

'We're police officers,' answered Inspector Savage. 'Who are you, sir?'

'I rent the shop down here,' said the

man. 'I heard a lot of tramping about and wondered what was happening. Police officers, you say, eh? What's the trouble?'

'Murder's the trouble,' said Mr. Budd, briefly.

The man's face changed. A startled look sprang into his rather deep-set eyes.

'Not Mrs. Loveridge?' he exclaimed.

'I'm afraid so,' said the big man.

'But — how did it happen? Who did it?' asked the owner of the shop.

'We can't answer any questions at present,' said Mr. Budd. 'I'd like to have a word with you later. What's your name, sir?'

'Snapper,' answered the other. 'William Snapper.'

'Yours is a lock-up shop, isn't it?' inquired the big man.

Mr. Snapper nodded.

'Yes,' he replied. 'I live in Brambleside Road. When did — when did it happen?'

'Durin' the night,' said Mr. Budd.

'Burglars, I suppose,' said Mr. Snapper. 'I wonder why they didn't break into my shop . . . '

'Surprisin', isn't it?' interrupted Mr.

61

Budd. 'There's no accountin' for what these crooks 'ull do. Have you got such a thing as a large screwdriver in your shop?'

'Yes,' answered Mr. Snapper looking rather surprised. 'Why?'

'I'd be obliged if you'd go an' fetch it,' said the stout superintendent. 'I'd like to borrow it for a minute if you wouldn't mind.'

Mr. Snapper nodded, opened his mouth to say something, thought better of it, and went away.

'We ought to be able to prise open the door with a screwdriver,' remarked Mr. Budd. 'It'll be easier than bustin' it open.'

It wasn't quite so easy as he imagined, however, for the door was a stout one and the screws firm in the solid frame. They managed it at last, under the astonished gaze of Mr. Snapper, and pushed the door open.

Inside there was a narrow passage similar to the one above. Both doors, opening off this passage, were wide open. One room, they could see, consisted of an office. It was plainly furnished with a large filing cabinet, a desk, several chairs, and a smaller desk. On both desks was a typewriter. As in the flat upstairs everything was in the greatest confusion. Papers and letters were strewn all over the floor, and the contents of the filing cabinet had been thrown in all directions.

Mr. Snapper, who had followed them in, gasped.

'Crikey!' he ejaculated. 'What a mess!'

Mr. Budd ignored him and looked about. His sleepy eyes were almost completely closed. For a moment, he stood still contemplating the chaotic litter. Then, after a moment, he suddenly became alert.

'Come on,' he snapped. 'Look through all this stuff an' see if you can find that copy of the play the dead woman mentioned in that bill. An' the manuscript, or whatever it was, she typed it from.'

Leek, Hoppy, and Inspector Savage began to sort through the papers and straighten out the mess. They worked methodically, examining every separate sheet.

Mr. Budd turned to William Snapper.

'Did you know Mrs. Loveridge well?' he asked.

'Pretty well,' answered Mr. Snapper. 'She wasn't a friend, if you know what I mean, but she'd been 'ere a long time an' we sort of 'ad a bit of a gossip now and again.'

'Did she employ any assistance in her business?' went on the big man. 'I see there's two machines . . . '

'Sometimes she did — when she was busy,' said Mr. Snapper. 'Only now 'an again, though. She didn't 'ave anyone workin' regularly for 'er.'

'Has she got a husband?'

'She 'ad but he's dead. He died in the war . . . '

'So she lived here alone?'

Mr. Snapper nodded.

'Between you an' me an' the gatepost,' he volunteered, 'she was a pretty lonely sort of woman altogether. Didn't go out much or have any friends come to see 'er.'

'How do you know?' asked Mr. Budd. 'You weren't here in the evening.'

'No, but she just gave me that impression,' said Mr. Snapper. 'You know how it is? You kind o' sense that sort of thing.'

'I see.' The big man nodded slowly. He understood perfectly what the other meant. You did get impressions about people sometimes and they were usually right.

'Terrible all these murders,' said Mr. Snapper, shaking his head. 'Lots of 'em these days. 'Specially women livin' alone. I suppose 'e was after any money that was lyin' around, eh? Can't understand why 'e didn't 'ave a go at my shop, though.'

He screwed up his face and shrugged his shoulders.

'Better get back, if you don't want me any more,' he said. 'Not much business about these days, but I'd best be there, just in case.'

Mr. Budd let him go. There was nothing more for the moment that Mr. Snapper could do to help them. Later, perhaps, he might have to be questioned again.

The litter was beginning to show some semblance of order but nothing in the nature of a play, either in typescript or manuscript, had come to light.

'I wasn't too sanguine that you'd find it,' said Mr. Budd, when the search of the office had been completed. 'There's the other room. Let's have a look in there.'

The other room was clearly used as a storeroom. All kinds of articles had been thrust in, old chairs, suitcases, piles of newspapers, any and almost every sort of junk. One glance showed them that this room had not been touched. There was no sign of anything having been moved nor any marks in the, quite appreciable, layer of dust that covered everything.

'He found what he wanted in the office,' grunted Mr. Budd. 'Well, there's still this feller Maitland. Maybe, we'll be luckier there.'

Hoppy looked at him curiously.

'I wonder what makes you so anxious to find this play?' he said, helping himself to one of his eternal Woodbines. 'Because the murderer was so keen on finding it, I suppose?'

'If a man is willin' to commit two murders to get hold of the manuscript of a play,' said Mr. Budd, 'it must be a very good one. I'm anxious to read this wonderful opus! We'll go along an' see this feller Maitland. Maybe, he'll let us read it.' He turned to Inspector Savage. 'I'd be glad,' he continued, 'if you'd have copies of the finger-prints of the dead man, Haines, sent along to the Yard . . . '

'Are you suggesting that he's in C.R.?' asked Hoppy.

'I'm not suggestin' anythin',' replied the big man. 'I just like to make sure o' things as I go along, that's all.'

5

Guy Maitland, under the imposing title of 'Mammoth Enterprises Ltd.', had a suite of offices in a large block just off Regent Street. A swift and silent lift whisked Mr. Budd, Sergeant Leek, and Hoppy to the fourth floor and they found the glass-panelled swing doors to the offices almost facing them when they got out.

The swing doors admitted them to a reception and inquiry office presided over by a willowy female, with a suitable face to match, who was seated behind a large bare desk on which was a small telephone switchboard.

This vision of loveliness surveyed them with a look of supreme condescension and disinterestedness. There was about her, under this mask, an air of excitement that she strove vainly to control.

'Mr. Maitland in, miss?' inquired Mr. Budd.

'I'm afraid,' replied the vision in an

ultra-refined voice, 'that Mr. Maitland can't see anybody at present.'

There was an underlying nervousness to the carefully cultivated tone. Mr. Budd produced his warrant card.

'The matter's urgent,' he said authoritatively. 'I must ask you to tell Mr. Maitland . . . '

He broke off, for at sight of his credentials the girl's manner changed. She dropped her acquired accent and spoke in her natural voice.

'Oh my Gawd!' she exclaimed. 'How many more of you?'

Mr. Budd looked at her in astonishment.

'In an' out all the time,' she went on. 'asking this an' wanting to know that . . . '

'Who?' demanded the big man sharply.

'The police, of course,' she retorted. 'There's one of 'em in the office now. Inspector Mac-somebody-or-other.'

'MacGregor,' exclaimed Mr. Budd. 'What on earth is he doin' here?'

Before the receptionist could answer this, the door of an inner room opened quickly and a tall, thin man, with a

69

rugged face and a short bristling moustache, appeared in the outer office.
Catching sight of Mr. Budd he stopped
dead on the threshold.

'What in thunder are ye doing here?' he
demanded in surprise. 'How did ye hear
aboot the mairder?'

'Whose murder?' asked the stout
superintendent. 'Don't you go tellin' me
that Guy Maitland has been . . . '

'Aye, he has,' replied Inspector
MacGregor. 'Mairdered during the airly
hours of this morning in his flat. That's
why I'm here . . . '

'Our friend is certainly a fast worker,'
murmured Mr. Budd.

'What was that ye said?' inquired
MacGregor suspiciously.

'Nothin',' said Mr. Budd. 'Are you in
charge of the case?'

Detective-Inspector MacGregor nodded.

'Aye,' he answered, 'an' I'd like to know
what brings you into it.'

'I think you an' me had better have a
little chat,' said Mr. Budd. 'Is there
anywhere here where we can be private?'

MacGregor looked at him. His face was

devoid of all expression. It might have been carved out of a piece of granite.

'Ye can come in the secretary's office,' he said. 'She'll noo doubt leave us alone for a wee while, if we ask her.'

He turned back into the room he had just left. Mr. Budd turned to Hoppy and Leek.

'You two stay here,' he said. 'An' don't you go tryin' out any of your pop singin'.'

'Can't I come in with you?' asked the reporter and Mr. Budd shook his head.

'Better not,' he answered. 'MacGregor can't stand reporters. He'd dance the highland fling, an' tear his hair oot by the roots, if you did.'

MacGregor re-appeared, followed by a pretty, dark girl with a troubled face and eyes that still showed traces of recent tears. She looked at them curiously as Inspector MacGregor beckoned Mr. Budd into the room she had just left.

'Now, sair,' said MacGregor closing the door. 'What is it ye wish to tell me?'

Mr. Budd explained. The big-boned Scotsman listened attentively with one bushy eyebrow raised in surprise.

71

'You see,' ended the stout superintendent, 'your case an' my case seem to be one case.'

'Aye, I mind what ye mean,' said the inspector. 'This man, Maitland, was killed in his bed some time in the airly hours of this morning. His head had been badly damaged by some kind of heavy weapon. We think it may have been a poker, or similar weapon, though we canna exactly tell at the moment what was used, ye understand . . .'

'Had the place been searched?' interrupted Mr. Budd quickly.

MacGregor shook his head.

'I wouldn't think so,' he said. 'There were noo signs of a sairch . . .'

'Did you find anythin' that looked like a play — either in typescript or manuscript?'

'Aye, there were several in the sitting-room,' answered the inspector.

'This particular one was called 'The Crime',' said the big man.

'I dinna recollect the titles of them. You mind, I wasna very interested,' said MacGregor, shaking his head. 'But ye can see for yoursel'. The dead man only lived a few streets away. In one of the new blocks of flats — terrible to look at from the outside but vairy comfortable when ye get in.'

'How did the murderer get in?' inquired the stout superintendent.

'There's a fire-escape that runs up the back to all the flats. One of these iron affairs . . . '

'The burglar's delight,' grunted Mr. Budd.

'Aye, ye may well call 'em that, sair,' agreed Inspector MacGregor. 'The kitchen window opens on to a wee platform. The mairderer had prised open the catch. It was an easy matter. It was the cleaner who made the discovery. A Mrs. Kennel. She came at the usual time in the morning but she couldn't make anybody hear . . . '

'Maitland lived alone?' interposed Mr. Budd.

'Aye,' went on MacGregor. 'He'd been married an' divorced four times an' this was between whiles, ye understand? Mrs. Kennel does the cleaning for another pairson in the flats an', thinking that Mr. Maitland was sleeping late, as he sometimes did, she went to this other pairson's fust. When she couldna get any reply the second time, she asked the porter to open the door with his master key. She found Maitland dead in his bed with his head all smashed in and sent for the p'lice . . . '

'And you were put in charge of the case?' remarked Mr. Budd. 'I see. Of course, they wouldn't know at the Yard that this murder had any connection with the one at Barnet. H'm. As I said before our killer has been a very busy little feller durin' the night.'

'Have ye a notion as to what's behind it, sair?' asked the inspector. 'It would appear to me that the mairderer was working against time . . . '

'You've hit it,' said Mr. Budd. 'Though why he should I haven't yet fathomed. Perhaps, if I can get a sight of this play I was talkin' about . . . '

'We'll go round to the flat noo,' said MacGregor.

'I'd like to have a word with the

secretary first,' objected Mr. Budd.

'Ye'll find her very helpful, though the poor lass has had a shock, ye mind. I'll call her in.'

MacGregor went over to the door and opened it.

'Will ye come in a moment, Miss Rider?' he called. 'The superintendent would like a word with ye.'

The dark girl came almost at once.

'I'm afraid, I can't tell you anything more,' she began, but Mr. Budd interrupted her.

'I think you'll be able to answer the questions I'm goin' to ask you, miss,' he said. 'Just sit down an' relax. This has been a shock to you, hasn't it?'

'It has rather,' she answered. 'You see, it was so unexpected . . . '

'Yes, of course,' went on the big man in his most soothing voice. 'It's very understandable that you should be upset. Now you make yourself comfortable an' I'll tell you what I want to know.'

The girl gave him a wintry smile and sat down at the desk.

'Now, miss,' said Mr. Budd, 'you were

Mr. Maitland's secretary, weren't you?'

She nodded.

'So you would handle all his letters an' parcels, wouldn't you?'

'I always attended to the mail, if that's what you mean,' she said.

'That's what I mean,' said Mr. Budd in his slow and ponderous way. 'Do you remember a registered packet arriving here yesterday?'

'We have quite a number of registered parcels,' she answered, frowning. 'Mr. — Mr. Maitland was always receiving plays from . . . '

'That's just what I'm talking about, miss,' broke in the big man. 'A play. The typescript of a play called 'The Crime'?'

Her face cleared.

'Oh, yes, I remember that,' she replied quickly. 'We had a letter about it on the previous day . . . '

'From a man named Jonathan Haines, eh?' asked Mr. Budd.

Again she nodded and her eyes were curious.

'How do you know that?' she said.

76

The stout superintendent ignored the question.

'Where is that play now?' he asked.

'Mr. Maitland took it home with him yesterday evening,' she answered.

'You're quite sure of that?'

'Yes, quite sure. He said he was going to read it.'

'You say that he used to get a lot of plays sent him,' said Mr. Budd.

'That's right,' she replied. 'He did . . . '

'Did he always read them at once?'

'No, of course not. He was a very busy man. He would not have had the time.'

'But he did with this partic'ler play,' said Mr. Budd, pouncing quickly on this point. 'Why did he do that?'

'Well, the author offered to finance the production,' she replied. 'That wasn't usual, you see. Of course, Mr. Maitland wouldn't have had anything to do with it if the play had been a bad one. That's why he was anxious to read it and see just what it was like.'

'I see,' murmured the big man. 'You didn't read it, I s'pose?'

'I wouldn't have the time,' she said. 'We

were very busy yesterday.'

'I think you've been very lucky,' remarked Mr. Budd.

'Very lucky indeed, miss.' He turned to MacGregor. 'That's all for the moment.'

Detective-Inspector MacGregor took his leave of Miss Rider and they passed into the outer office where the Queen of the Reception Desk was talking to Hoppy. Leek, staring unhappily out of the window, turned as they came in.

'Did you find anythin'?' he asked.

'A little,' answered Mr. Budd. 'We're goin' along to Maitland's flat. I think we're too late, but there's just a chance.'

'Too late for what?' asked the sergeant.

'Too late for what I'd like to find there,' said the stout superintendent. 'Come on, Hopkins.'

The reporter stubbed out the butt of his cigarette, took out another one from a packet and lit it.

'You remember me, don't you, MacGregor?' he asked as they descended in the lift. 'I gave you that write-up in *The Messenger* when you were on the Calcroft case.'

'Aye, I remember ye,' answered the inspector shortly. 'A more persistent young mon I've never had to deal with.'

Hoppy grinned.

'We newspaper men have to be persistent if we want to live,' he said.

'I canna see any reason for that,' snapped MacGregor.

'He can be quite useful sometimes,' put in Mr. Budd.

'Thank you for those few kind words,' cried Hoppy. 'After years of selfish endeavour I have at last achieved the appreciation that I deserve!'

'Not from me ye haven't,' said MacGregor dourly.

'Even your granite heart will melt in time,' retorted Hoppy. 'Here we are.'

The lift came to a smooth stop and they got out.

'Not worth taking the car,' said MacGregor as they came out on to the pavement. 'It's only a wee step.'

'We'll take the car,' said Mr. Budd firmly. 'I don't believe in exercise when there's no need.'

'Hence the waistline,' remarked Hoppy.

'You could do with a little less fat.'

'So could you,' retorted Mr. Budd. 'About the head!'

They got into the police car and, after a few seconds, got out again. The journey, as MacGregor had said, was only a 'wee step'.

Guy Maitland's flat was one of those luxurious dwellings that never appear to have been lived in. Its appointments were expensive, but had obviously been provided by a firm of interior decorators. There was no personal element at all. The place was very neat. Not even a chair seemed to be out of place.

The body of the dead man had been removed for the autopsy, but Inspector MacGregor showed Mr. Budd the bedroom where the crime had been committed. The stout superintendent glanced quickly round, but he was obviously not very interested.

'I'd like to have a look at these plays you was talkin' about,' he said. 'In the sittin'-room, you said, didn't you?'

The inspector nodded and conducted him into an adjoining room. It was a large room with several deep easy chairs, a large cocktail cabinet, a television set, and a thick pile carpet that covered the floor from wall to wall. Here, again, there was the impression that the place was only for show and that no one had used it. There was a large desk with nothing on it but a leather blotter, a calendar, and a cut-glass inkstand on a silver tray. On a small table, however, beside the desk were several typed manuscripts, neatly bound and stacked.

Mr. Budd went to them quickly and peered at each one. When he had gone through the lot, he pursed his lips.

'Nothin' to interest me,' he said, disappointedly. 'I was afraid there wouldn't be. Did Maitland have a tape-recorder?'

'We didna see anything of the kind,' said MacGregor. 'We made a pretty thorough sairch of the whole flat.'

'Most likely he didn't,' grunted Mr. Budd. He plucked thoughtfully at his lower lip with a finger and thumb. 'Oh, well,' he went on at length, 'there's nothin' more we can do here. Since both seem to be on different portions of the same case we'd better keep in touch, eh?'

'I'd be glad of any help you can give me, sair,' said MacGregor with as much gratitude as his stolid nature would allow to appear. 'It would seem to be a vurry curious business — vurry curious.'

He gave Mr. Budd a sharp glance from his narrow eyes, but the stout superintendent was not to be drawn. Whatever he thought about the case in the inmost recesses of his mind, remained there.

He took his leave of Detective-Inspector MacGregor and went slowly back to the waiting police car with Leek and Hoppy.

'What do we do now?' asked the reporter, fishing a Woodbine out of his packet and lighting it.

'I'm goin' back to the Yard,' replied Mr. Budd, settling himself comfortably in a corner of the back seat. 'Can I drop you anywhere?'

'I see,' said Hoppy. 'This is where I get the order of the boot, eh?'

'You can call it that, if you like,' grunted the big man, closing his eyes wearily. 'An' just you listen to me. When you print an account o' this business in that rag of yours, you're not to mention anythin' about this play, you understand? Not a single hint that we know anythin' about it.'

'All right,' agreed Hoppy. 'But I'd like to know why?'

'Maybe when I know meself I'll tell you,' said Mr. Budd. 'Now, don't you forget — not a single word, or there'll be trouble.'

Hoppy grinned. He knew that it was no good arguing with the stout superintendent. When the time was ripe, Mr. Budd would give him the story and it would probably be an exclusive. The big man always played fair.

They dropped Hoppy near the Strand to make his way to Fleet Street, and continued on to the Yard.

When Mr. Budd reached his little office he sat down behind his desk with a sigh of relief.

'Will you be wantin' me for a bit?' asked Leek hopefully.

'Well,' remarked Mr. Budd, settling

himself more comfortably in his chair, 'you haven't done much up to now, have you?'

'I've bin watchin' points,' said the lean sergeant. 'I've got the whole thing in me head . . .'

'Oh you have, have you,' grunted his superior. 'Well, what d'you make of it, eh?'

Leek fidgeted with his feet.

'It wants a good bit o' thinkin' about,' he said. 'There's a lot I don't understand . . .'

'You surprise me,' broke in Mr. Budd sarcastically. 'I should've thought you'd've got it all cut an' dried by now, an' ready to go off an' arrest the murderer. Is that why you wanted to know if I wanted you? So's you could get crackin'?'

'You will 'ave yer little joke,' answered Leek with a feeble smile. 'I thought I'd like to go an' get a bite to eat. I ain't had any lunch . . .'

'Neither have I,' retorted Mr. Budd. 'But, of course, I'm not trainin' to be a pop singer! I'm only doin' the job I get paid for, tryin' to catch thieves an' murderers. Go on, go an' lubricate your tonsils so that your future fans won't be disappointed . . . '

'You never did take me seriously,' broke in the injured Leek. 'You oughter be glad that I've found me proper sphere at last . . . '

'Ever since I've known you,' snarled Mr. Budd, 'you've been dreamin' up some wildcat scheme to avoid workin'.'

'You 'ave to work pretty hard to become a pop singer,' expostulated Leek.

'Then you'll never become one!' snorted the big man. 'Go an' find some food, but be back here in an hour. I've got a call to make an' I'm taking you with me . . . '

'Where?' demanded the sergeant.

'We're goin' to call on an actress,' said Mr. Budd, 'so try an' behave yourself.'

Leek shambled to the door. Just as he was going out, Superintendent Nicholls of the Criminal Record Office almost knocked him over as he entered hastily.

'Oh, sorry,' he apologised. 'I say, Budd, what have you got hold of?'

'What d'you mean, what have I got

hold of?' asked the stout man, regarding him sleepily.

'Where did you get those dabs you sent us?' demanded Nicholls.

'From the fingers of a dead man at Barnet,' answered Mr. Budd. 'His name was Jonathan Haines an' he was murdered last night.'

'That's what he called himself, did he?' said Nicholls. 'That isn't the name we knew him by here.' He tapped a bulky folder he was carrying under his arm. 'Do you remember John Gilmore who got fifteen years for robbery and manslaughter . . . ?'

Mr. Budd, suddenly alert, hoisted himself up in his chair.

'He escaped from Dartmoor prison six months ago,' he said. 'That the feller you mean?'

'Yes.' Nicholls nodded. 'That's your Jonathan Haines,' he said.

6

'I s'pose you're quite sure of that?' said Mr. Budd, rubbing his chin gently.

'Oh quite,' replied Nicholls. He tapped the folder again. 'I've got it all here, fingerprints, photographs, the whole story.'

He pulled up a chair and put the folder down on the desk. Leek, who had been hovering uncertainly by the door, ventured a remark.

'Can I still go an' get a bite?' he asked dolefully.

'I didn't even know you was still there,' said Mr. Budd. 'Go an' bite away to your heart's content.'

The lean sergeant went out, shutting the door behind him.

'Now then, let's see what you've got there,' went on the stout superintendent. 'It should be interestin'.'

Nicholls opened the folder and took our several photographs and cards of fingerprints.

'These are Gilmore's,' he said passing them over to Mr. Budd. 'And these are the dabs you sent me. You don't have to be an expert to see that they're the same.'

Mr. Budd peered at them. As Nicholls said, there was no doubt. Gilmore and Haines had been one and the same man. If there *had* been the smallest room for error, the police photographs would have instantly dispelled it. The pictures of Gilmore were identical with the dead man.

'It certainly seems pretty conclusive,' grunted Mr. Budd.

'Can't say I remember Gilmore's case in detail. It happened a long time ago . . .'

'Eight years almost,' put in Nicholls.

'Somethin' to do with the shootin' of a money-lender, wasn't it?'

'That's right. A man named Wurtz was shot, and Gilmore was accused of the crime. The evidence was pretty strong against him but the jury disagreed and brought in a verdict of manslaughter. It's all there — in that folder.'

'I'd like to go through it,' said Mr.

Budd. 'It might give me the clue I'm lookin' for.'

'Carry on,' said Nicholls. 'I'll leave it with you. Send it back to C.R. when you've finished.'

He got up.

'The police are still looking for Gilmore,' he said. 'We'd better tell 'em they needn't bother any more.'

'I'll attend to that,' said the big man. 'Thanks for the trouble, Nicholls.'

'All in the day's work,' grinned Nicholls and took his departure.

Mr. Budd took one of his evil-smelling, black cigars from his waistcoat pocket and lit it with great satisfaction. Blowing out clouds of acrid smoke that resembled a combination of burning tar and linoleum, he pulled the folder nearer to him and settled down comfortably to read.

Joseph Wurtz, a registered money-lender, who conducted his business from an office in Bond Street, returned to his private residence in Berkhamsted earlier than usual one evening. After dining at seven-thirty, he retired to his study, telling his manservant, a man named Neate, that he was expecting a visitor who would give no name but was to be shown in to him immediately he arrived.

The manservant was used to this kind of thing and therefore saw nothing unusual in these instructions. His employer was in the habit of interviewing several of his more important clients at his private residence after business hours. When, an hour later, the expected visitor arrived, he was conducted at once to the study.

About ten minutes later, Wurtz rang for Neate and ordered refreshments to be brought in. This order Neate hastened to obey.

As he laid down the tray on a table near the desk, he saw in front of his employer a very thick wad of five-pound notes that must have represented a large sum of money. He withdrew and went back to his quarters near the kitchen. A quarter of an hour later, he heard the muffled sound of two shots, fired in rapid succession, from the direction of the study.

Running to the study door he threw it

open and saw his employer sprawled across the desk, the blood spouting from a wound in his head. Standing staring at him with a stunned expression on his face was the visitor who had been with him earlier in the evening, holding in his hand a revolver.

The sound of the shots had brought the other servants on the scene. Neate put the unknown visitor in charge of the chauffeur and rang up the police.

The man, who gave his name as John Gilmore, seemed completely dazed when he was charged, later, with the murder of the moneylender. He told a rambling and entirely incoherent story.

He affirmed that while he was still talking to Wurtz, the French window was suddenly flung violently open and a man had burst across the threshold. This man had shot Wurtz, thrown down the revolver, and made off. Gilmore said that he had picked up the weapon and fired at the retreating figure of the murderer, but his shot had gone wide. He was deciding whether or not to follow the man, when Neate had burst into the room.

The story was a very thin one. One of the bullets had hit the window frame and this, and the one extracted from the dead moneylender, were, later, found to have been fired from the gun in Gilmore's possession. Another fact which seemed to clinch the evidence against him was that the only fingerprints on the revolver were his own.

The motive, too, was evident. The money, which Neate swore he had seen on the desk in front of his master, was found in Gilmore's pockets when he was searched. He stated that it was his own. He swore that he had brought it with him to repay a loan which he owed to Wurtz. But this was proved to be a complete fabrication. An examination of the dead moneylender's books and accounts showed no transaction with any person of the name of Gilmore.

The police were convinced from the beginning that Gilmore was guilty. He could give no description of the man who was supposed to have burst in through the French windows. He said he wore a heavy overcoat and that a muffler covered the entire lower part of his face. The whole story appeared so unlikely that they discounted it. Their theory was that Gilmore had been refused a loan from Wurtz and in a fit of temper had shot the moneylender and snatched up the money — a sum amounting to five thousand pounds. The *two* shots, they suggested, had been fired because Wurtz had ducked, avoiding the first one, which had struck the window-frame. In spite of the fact that the accused man stuck stubbornly to his story and protested his innocence, he was eventually committed for trial.

The trial was a short one. The jury disagreed and, to the surprise of the prosecution, brought in a verdict of manslaughter.

John Gilmore was sentenced to fifteen years and that was the end of the case. He was sent to Dartmoor and remained there for eight years.

And then he escaped.

During a fog which suddenly descended on the stone quarries where he was working, he managed to make a get-away.

That was the gist of the story. Until the murder of Jonathan Haines in Barnet, John Gilmore had completely vanished.

Mr. Budd closed the folder and laid the stub of his cigar in the ashtray. With great deliberation, he fished in his pocket for another, sniffed at it delicately, and lit it with care. Then he leaned back in his chair and closed his eyes.

So the dead man at Barnet who had called himself Jonathan Haines had been John Gilmore a suspected murderer and an escaped convict. Well, that was a step further, but where did it get him? With the pungent smoke from his cigar wreathing about his head, Mr. Budd considered this.

Somebody had considered it very urgent that Gilmore should die. Not only this, they had also had the same idea concerning Phyllida Loveridge and Guy Maitland. In this connection the play that Gilmore had written seemed to be the link. Where could you go from there? It seemed reasonable to suppose that the play was dangerous to this unknown person who had killed three times to get hold of it.

Why?

A cone of ash dropped on to Mr. Budd's capacious stomach but he was too absorbed in his thoughts to notice it.

Supposing Gilmore had been speaking the truth?

Supposing there *had* been a man at the window who had shot Wurtz? What then?

Well, that would mean that Gilmore had suffered a long term of imprisonment for a crime that he never committed. That wouldn't make him any too pleased with life. In fact, he'd feel bitter and angry and generally mixed up. Now, supposing that, when he escaped, his one thought was to find the man who had shot Wurtz and prove his innocence, and supposing that he had succeeded? Supposing that this man had become aware that Gilmore had discovered his identity? That would supply a pretty strong motive for Gilmore's — or Haines as he called himself — murder.

Mr. Budd sighed. There was, he admitted to himself, a great deal of supposing about this idea. But that was the way you got somewhere. Just keep on supposing until you got it right. There were a lot of snags in his theory. For instance, how had Gilmore succeeded in finding the unknown man? He couldn't have known who he was beforehand or he would have said so at his trial . . .

Besides he hadn't spent his time after his escape from prison looking for anybody. He'd written a play.

Yes.

And it was because of that play that Loveridge and Maitland had died. The play was dangerous to the murderer . . .

Mr. Budd experienced that odd sensation, which most people have experienced in their time, of almost grasping a nebulous idea, of seeing the whirling fragments drop neatly into their proper places, and then losing them before they formed a coherent picture.

Still, he had got a *little* further . . .

It was a quarter-past six when the melancholy Leek put in an appearance.

'I hope,' remarked Mr. Budd, eyeing him critically, 'that you've had enough bites to keep you goin' for a bit?'

96

'I only 'ad a coffee an' a sandwich,' answered Leek. 'I've been listenin' to Danny Drooling's latest record. It's a smasher!'

'Is it?' grunted Mr. Budd. 'That's the only thing all the ones I've heard are fit for — smashing . . . '

'He sends you,' exclaimed Leek enthusiastically.

'He seems to've sent you off your rocker,' snapped the big man. 'You'd better come back to earth. We're goin' to the theatre.'

Leek's long face brightened.

'Arty Languish is on at the Palace,' he said eagerly. ''E's just made a new record 'I Wander Alone . . . '.'

'An' I'm not surprised,' said Mr. Budd. 'I saw him once an' that's the best thing he could do. We're not goin' to the theatre for fun, we're goin' on business.'

'Oh!' muttered the disappointed Leek. 'Where are we goin' then?'

'We're goin' to the Majestic Theatre to see Miss Janice Sheridan,' answered Mr. Budd. 'An' she isn't a pop singer. She's an actress an' from all accounts a very good one.' He got heavily to his feet and dusted the ash from his waistcoat. 'I'm goin' to grab a sandwich,' he continued, 'an' then I'll be ready. Don't you go beetlin' off anywhere. An' don't go practisin' any pop songs, or we'll be gettin' complaints.'

He left the office and went down to the entrance. There was a small teashop round the corner in Whitehall where they knew him rather well. He ordered two rounds of ham sandwich and a pot of strong tea, realizing that he had had nothing to eat or drink since his breakfast. He ate his sandwiches, drank two cups of tea, and went back to pick up Leek.

The stage doorkeeper at the Majestic Theatre shook his head when the big man inquired for Miss Sheridan.

'She ain't come in yet,' he said curtly, 'an' I don't suppose she'll see anyone when she does.'

'She'll see me,' replied Mr. Budd, and held out his warrant card.

The old man peered at it suspiciously through his steel-rimmed spectacles.

'The police, are yer?' he grunted.

'Well, part of 'em,' admitted Mr. Budd.

'There's been another feller after Miss Sheridan,' volunteered the doorkeeper. 'What's it all about, eh?'

'Another feller, eh?' said Mr. Budd with interest. 'What was his name?'

'Hopkins,' said the old man. 'Somethin' to do with the newspapers, 'e is . . . '

'He's been here, 'as he?' murmured the stout superintendent. 'He don't let the grass get much time to grow . . . '

'Hello, hello,' cried a cheery voice behind him. 'The great Budd himself! And I don't mean anything personal.'

Hoppy, the inevitable Woodbine drooping from his mouth, grinned happily as Mr. Budd swung round.

'Thought I'd follow up the clue of the mysterious photograph,' he continued. 'I see you had the same idea.'

'It was a pretty obvious one,' said Mr. Budd.

'Granted,' agreed Hoppy. 'Well, now we can join forces again.'

'Now, look here, young Hopkins,' began Mr. Budd, 'I don't . . . '

At that moment the stage door opened and a girl came in quickly. She was of medium height, fair, with an attractive smile that seemed to light up her rather deep blue eyes. She looked quickly at them and then spoke to the old door-keeper.

'Good evening, Japp,' she said. 'Any letters?'

'No, Miss Sheridan,' he answered, 'but these people wants to see you.'

'I'm afraid I can't see anybody now,' she replied. 'I'm late already . . . '

'I won't keep you long, miss,' interposed Mr. Budd. He introduced himself and the girl's eyes widened.

'Is it urgent?' she asked. 'I really haven't much time . . . '

'I just want to ask you one or two questions,' said the big man. 'It'll help the police a lot if you can answer them.'

Janice Sheridan frowned and hesitated.

'It's very awkward,' she said. 'I really *am* in a hurry . . . ' Suddenly she made up her mind. 'Very well. Come through to my dressing-room. I can spare you five minutes.'

She led the way along a narrow corridor to a room at the end. It was occupied by an elderly woman who was brushing a pair of shoes.

Janice ushered them in, threw off her coat, and sat down in front of her dressing-table.

'Now,' she said lighting a cigarette, 'tell me what you want to know, and please be quick.'

'Are you acquainted with anyone of the name of Jonathan Haines?' asked Mr. Budd without preamble.

The girl looked surprised. She blew out a thin cloud of smoke and there was a slight pause before she replied. Then she said:

'It's rather curious you should ask that.'

'Why?' asked Mr. Budd.

'It reminds me of a rather extraordinary incident that has been puzzling me for some time.'

'What was that, miss?' asked the big man.

'It happened about three months ago,' she answered. 'I hadn't long been in the West End but I'd been lucky and was getting a lot of publicity in the newspapers. One night, when I got to the theatre, there was a letter for me. It was from this person you mention, Jonathan Haines. He asked me if I could send him a photograph of myself. I shouldn't have done so except that he said he had been a great friend of my father.'

'Where did you send this photograph?'

'King's Lodge in Barnet . . . '

'Did you remember the name, miss? Jonathan Haines?'

She shook her head.

'You never met this man, Haines?'

'No. But three days after I sent the photograph I received another letter from him. It was a most extraordinary letter. He thanked me for the photograph and asked if I would keep a small key that he enclosed. He asked if I would do this in memory of my father and would I carry it always with me. He said I would know what to do with the key because, in the event of his death, I was to follow the instructions in a sealed letter that would reach me.'

'That's very interestin',' remarked Mr.

Budd. 'Have you got this key, miss?'

'Yes, it's in my bag.' She reached for her handbag and opened it. She took out a crumpled envelope which she held out to the stout superintendent. He took it and opened it.

'That is the letter,' she said. 'The key is with it.'

Mr. Budd drew out a sheet of paper and a small key. It was about two inches long and was made of steel. His face was expressionless as he turned it about in his podgy fingers. After a moment he put it down on his broad knee and smoothed out the letter. It was written in a queer kind of backward hand and began without the usual address and date:

'*My dear Miss Sheridan,*
   '*I must convey my thanks for the photograph which you so very kindly sent me. I am taking the liberty of asking you a further favour. I want you to take charge of the enclosed key, keeping it always in your personal possession. I ask you to do this in memory of your father. In the event of*

my death a sealed envelope will reach you explaining this request and instructing you how to use the key.

Yours very sincerely,

Jonathan Haines'.

Mr. Budd refolded the letter. He said:

'Did your father ever mention Jonathan Haines?'

She shook her head with a faint smile.

'I wouldn't remember,' she replied. 'You see, my father died when I was a child.'

'I see,' said Mr. Budd. 'Maybe, your mother would remember, miss?'

The girl's face hardened suddenly.

'My mother is dead too,' she answered. 'She died five years ago.'

Mr. Budd nodded thoughtfully.

'What are all these questions about?' asked Janice curiously. 'What are you trying to find out?'

'I'm tryin' to find out who murdered Jonathan Haines last night, miss,' announced the big man abruptly.

Janice Sheridan gave a violent start.

'Murdered him?' she exclaimed. 'Is he . . . ?'

'I'm afraid he is, miss,' interrupted Mr. Budd. 'His name wasn't Haines either. He was a man named John Gilmore, a convict under sentence for robbery and manslaughter, who escaped from prison a few months ago. Does the name, Gilmore mean anything to you?'

She frowned and slowly shook her head.

'Not a thing,' she declared. 'I don't understand why he should have . . . '

There was a resounding knock on the door and a youthful voice cried: 'Quarter of an hour, Miss Sheridan.'

Janice got up quickly.

'I'm afraid you'll have to go now,' she said. 'I must get made up and dressed.'

'That's all right, miss,' said Mr. Budd. 'I'd like to see you tomorrow if possible . . . '

'I shall be in my flat all the morning,' she broke in. 'I should like to hear more about this murder. I've been puzzled about the key . . . '

'Ah, the key,' said the stout superintendent. 'I'd like to take that with me, miss.'

'Do,' she agreed. 'Now, please, you

really must go . . . '

They took their leave of the girl and left the theatre.

'Well?' said Hoppy, as Mr. Budd walked to the waiting car. 'What do you make of that, eh? What's that key, and why did this man, Gilmore, send it to Janice Sheridan?'

'I'd like to be able to tell you,' replied the big man. 'Queer, isn't it? I might make a guess what the key is for, but I can't imagine why he should have picked out Miss Sheridan to send it to.'

'Unless he really *was* a friend of her father's,' said Hoppy. 'You surprised me when you told her all that stuff about Gilmore. I suppose I can't print that?'

'You suppose rightly,' said Mr. Budd. 'If you print a word about it yet, I'll have you on the carpet.'

'Pity,' grunted Hoppy. 'It'ud make a good scoop. Where are you going now?'

'Back to the Yard,' answered Mr. Budd, 'an' then I'm goin' home.'

He got ponderously into the police car and waited for Leek to follow, but the lean sergeant hesitated.

'Will you be wantin' me for anythin'?' he asked.

'Meanin', I suppose,' growled Mr. Budd, 'that you want to go off on the loose, eh?'

'I thought I might pop inter the Palace,' mumbled Leek.

'To see this Droolin' feller, eh?' remarked the stout superintendent disparagingly. 'Venus in blue jeans. Bah!'

''I feel funny all over',' said Leek.

'You look it,' snapped Mr. Budd.

'That's the title of Danny Drooling's latest hit,' interposed Hoppy with a grin.

'Most appropriate,' commented Mr. Budd. 'All right, get along an' waste your time. But don't you turn up late in the mornin'. There's a lot to be done.'

Leek nodded and drifted away.

Hoppy chuckled.

'He's got the pop fever badly,' he said.

'He's always gettin' somethin' badly,' grunted Mr. Budd. 'Except a capacity for work. That's never got him at all.'

'He's done some quite good work, you know,' said the reporter. 'You've admitted that yourself.'

'He's not so bad,' said Mr. Budd a little grudgingly. 'He *will* keep gettin' all these wild ideas an' hare-brained schemes. Can you imagine him as a pop singer?'

'I don't see how he could be much worse than some of 'em,' remarked Hoppy. 'Well, I'll be off. Can I come with you to see Janice Sheridan in the morning?'

'I suppose you can,' said Mr. Budd without enthusiasm. 'I'll be at the Yard at ten.'

The police car drove off, and Hoppy, lighting a Woodbine, went off to get himself a meal at a nearby café.

When Mr. Budd reached his cheerless office, he found the plaster casts of the footprints and hand, that he had asked for, on his desk. Their appearance was rather startling. Each cast represented a perfect semblance of a white shoe, surprisingly complete in every detail so far as the soles were concerned. Even the arrangement of the nails was plainly visible.

But if the appearance of the shoe casts was striking, that of the hand was even more so. It looked positively uncanny. The effect was that of a snowy hand with outstretched, clutching fingers. The fine, sandy soil had yielded a wealth of detail. The creases and lines of the palm were all perfectly clear and distinct. There were even traces of the ridges on the fingertips.

Mr. Budd examined them with interest and then locked them carefully away in a drawer of his desk. He gave a prodigious yawn, lighted one of his acrid cigars, and made his way down to the entrance. His own dilapidated little car, which was a standing joke among his *confrères*, was parked in the quadrangle. Hoisting himself into the driving seat, he started the engine, and drove to his small villa in Streatham.

His housekeeper, a dour woman in whom the big man lived in constant dread, greeted him with the announcement that his meal would be ready in half an hour.

Mr. Budd went up to his bedroom and got into a dressing-gown. Coming down to the little dining-room, he poured himself out a John Haig from the bottle on the sideboard, and settled himself in the big easy chair by the electric fire.

He had brought the little key which Gilmore had sent Janice Sheridan back with him, and he turned it about in his podgy fingers. He thought that he could guess what it opened and, a more wild guess, what it guarded. To turn his guess into fact would take a great deal of time and a certain amount of trouble. But the result might prove to be worth it.

His housekeeper came in to lay the table, and gave an audible and disapproving sniff as she saw the dressing-gown. She strongly disapproved of any form of coddling or self-indulgence. Any form of comfort, according to her, was pandering to the senses and definitely decadent. But she was, not withstanding these peculiarities, a kind woman according to her lights, and genuinely fond of and loyal to her employer. There had been a time, when Mr. Budd had been seriously ill with pneumonia, when she had gone without sleep for several nights, and worn herself to a shadow, to nurse him.

Mr. Budd ate his meal slowly and with

enjoyment. In spite of his bulk he was not a large eater. Indeed, there were many days when he subsisted on nothing more than tea and toast, too busy to find the time for a more substantial meal. But he never found that it did him any harm. When he had consumed the portion of treacle tart which concluded his meal, he went back to his chair with the large cup of coffee which she brought him.

Lighting one of his black cigars, which even the protestations of his housekeeper had never succeeded in stopping, he lay back in his chair and closed his eyes.

Carefully and methodically, he went over in his mind the events of the day. It was at these moments that his really brilliant brain was at its keenest. He allowed his mind to peer and probe among the scattered fragments of the particular problem that was occupying his attention, sorting facts and weaving theories until he saw a way through the maze to a solution.

A vague idea was worrying at his mind. It was hazy and embryonic but might become clearer from concentration.

He went carefully over the facts as he knew them.

Some three months ago a man calling himself Jonathan Haines writes a letter to Janice Sheridan asking for a photograph of herself and stating that he was a friend of her father's. She sends him the photograph. Shortly after, Janice Sheridan gets another letter. With the letter is a small key which she is asked to keep always in her personal possession. As an inducement for her to agree, Haines again mentions that he was a friend of her father's, and goes on to say that in the event of his death, will she use the key in accordance with the instructions he has left in a sealed envelope.

Haines is murdered one night at his house in Barnet where he has been living the life of a hermit. It is learned from his housekeeper that he has been engaged in writing a play. But there are no traces of this play among his effects. Neither, although there is a tape-recorder, are there any tapes. The housekeeper remembers posting a parcel to a Miss Phyllida Loveridge in Barnet High Street. Phyllida

Loveridge turns out to be a typist, but she is found murdered in similar circumstances to Haines. Among the papers in her flat is found a bill, made out ready to send to Haines, that shows that she has typed two copies of a play entitled 'The Crime.' It also shows that one of these copies has been sent to a well-known theatrical producer named Guy Maitland. This man is also murdered in his flat. There is no trace of the play, either in Phyllida Loveridge's office and flat, or at Maitland's. All the copies of the play have vanished and there seems little doubt that the murderer not only took them but was *looking* for them.

It is then discovered that Jonathan Haines was not Jonathan Haines at all but a man named John Gilmore, suspected of murdering a moneylender called Joseph Wurtz, and a convict who has recently escaped from prison.

Mr. Budd slowly opened his eyes. This was a pretty fair résumé of the sequence of events. Where did it get him?

One thing seemed clear. The motive for the three murders was the play. The murderer had killed to get hold of that play — to get hold of *all* the copies that existed. And not only that. He had killed all the people, so far as he was aware, *who had read it and knew what it was about.*

Mr. Budd dropped the butt of his cigar into an ashtray and got heavily to his feet.

He decided to call it a day.

7

Janice Sheridan was never very late in the morning. She usually had her breakfast brought to her on a tray at half-past eight and was bathed and dressed by half-past nine.

On the morning after Mr. Budd's visit to the Majestic Theatre she was a little later than usual. She had not slept very well because her mind was puzzling over the death of the man who had sent her the key. The whole thing was exciting and intriguing. Why had this man sent the key to her? What was it, and what was she supposed to do with it? Now that he was dead she should be in receipt of the letter of instructions he had mentioned. Where was that coming from? Certainly Gilmore couldn't be sending it himself so he must have arranged for it to be sent after his death. But who was going to send it?

Janice wondered if this had occurred to the detective who had come to see her at the theatre. She would suggest it to him when he came that morning. Perhaps, Gilmore had a solicitor to whom he had given the letter.

She picked up the morning paper and the first thing that caught her eye was a glaring headline splashed across the top of the front page:

MYSTERIOUS MURDER OF RECLUSE

Man found Stabbed to Death in Lonely House at Barnet.

The account that followed contained only the briefest facts of the discovery.

Janice was in the middle of reading the few lurid details when the telephone rang. Getting up, she went over and took the receiver off its rack.

'Hello?' she said and was interrupted before she could say any more by an urgent voice at the other end of the wire: 'Is that Miss Sheridan?' it inquired. 'Listen, Miss Sheridan. I'm speaking for Mr. Webster . . . '

'Oh, yes,' said Janice. Clive Webster was

the stage director of her play at the Majestic Theatre. 'What is it?'

'Travis Manners has been taken ill,' said the voice. 'His understudy will have to play tonight. Mr. Webster wants you to come down to the theatre at once so that you can rehearse your scenes with him. A car is being sent to pick you up.'

'Oh, I am sorry — about Travis,' said Janice. 'I'll be ready in a few minutes.'

She called her maid and hastily explained.

'Mr. Crosse was coming to take me to lunch,' she said. 'Will you tell him to meet me at the theatre?'

The maid nodded.

'And there's a superintendent from Scotland Yard supposed to be coming this morning,' went on Janice hurriedly. 'Explain what has happened, will you, Alice?'

The maid looked a little surprised but promised that she would. Janice put on her coat and collected her handbag.

'I don't know what time I shall be back,' she said as she hastily powdered her nose in front of the mirror. 'Ask the superintendent to ring and make another appointment.'

There was a ring at the door of the flat.

'I'll go,' said Janice, as the maid was moving toward the door. 'I expect it's the car.'

A tall man in a chauffeur's uniform stood on the threshold as she opened the door.

'Miss Sheridan?' he said.

'You've come from Mr. Webster?' she said and he nodded. They went down in the lift and crossed the pavement to a large saloon that stood at the entrance to the block of flats. The chauffeur opened the door and she got in. The man closed the door, got in the front behind the wheel, and they drove off.

Janice leaned back in the corner of the seat and frowned. She was a little worried. She had got used to playing opposite Manners. It was going to be disconcerting to adjust herself to the personality of the understudy however good he was.

She became so occupied with her thoughts that she never troubled to look at the streets they were passing along, until the atmosphere of the car began to get so oppressive that she leaned forward to open one of the windows.

Then she noticed that the car was travelling in the wrong direction!

They were going away from the Majestic Theatre!

She tapped on the window dividing her from the driver, but he took no notice. She tried again but still, he remained at the wheel, deaf to her signals.

Janice felt suddenly frightened.

It flashed into her mind that this man had never come from Webster — that the telephone call hadn't come from him either . . .

An unaccountable feeling of drowsiness swept over her. She tried to fight it with all her willpower but the car, the streets, the figure of the man at the wheel, became misty and blurred. Dark splashes danced in front of her eyes. With a desperate effort she tried to pull at the handle of the window . . . But consciousness was slipping away from her . . . Her senses swam. Fighting off curtains of dense velvety blackness, she slumped back against the cushions and what was left of her senses slipped away . . .

⋆   ⋆   ⋆

She opened her eyes to find herself lying on a soft settee in a dimly-lighted room. The light came from a green-shaded reading-lamp on a large writing-table in the middle of the room.

Her head throbbed and her throat felt dry. She felt sick. Her eyes hurt and felt as though they were full of sand. As she began to recover the full use of her senses, she moaned faintly and tried to move. The effort redoubled the throbbing in her head and she was forced to close her eyes again. For some minutes she lay in semi-consciousness, vaguely under the impression that she must be dreaming.

Gradually, as her dazed brain began to clear, she remembered. The message from the theatre; the ride in the big saloon; the faintness that had overcome her . . .

As she realised their significance, she

struggled up into a sitting position and stared about her.

The exertion made her head swim, but she set her teeth and fought off the faintness. She was in a large, oblong room, comfortably furnished as a library. The settee, on which she had been lying, was drawn up in front of an electric fire that threw out a warm glow. A clock ticked steadily on the mantelpiece. It was half-past two!

The curtains were drawn over two big windows to shut out any possible view of the outside world. Where was she?

Janice rose unsteadily to her feet with the intention of going over and pulling back the curtains, but she found that she was too weak, and had to sink back on the settee. Presently, she felt better and tried again. She was halfway over to the window nearest to her when there was a click from the door and she looked round, startled.

The door opened and a man came in quickly. He was the driver who had called for her, but he had discarded his chauffeur's uniform.

'You've recovered, eh?' he said in a low, gruff voice, closing the door and coming towards her. 'You can come away from those windows. There's nothing to see.'

'Who are you? Why have you brought me here?' demanded Janice.

'The first question is no concern of yours,' answered the man shortly. 'I've brought you here because you have something I want. A key.'

So that was it!

'What key?' she asked.

'Don't pretend you don't know,' he said. 'I know it was sent to you. Give it me.'

'I haven't got it,' she answered.

'It's no use telling me lies,' began the other.

'I'm not,' she interrupted. Her heart was beating fast, but her voice was without a tremor. 'The key is no longer in my possession.'

The man muttered something under his breath. Stepping quickly to her he gripped her by the wrist.

'What have you done with it?' he snarled. 'Quick, tell me.'

'I gave it to the police,' she answered calmly.

He raised his hand and she thought he was going to hit her, and flinched.

'You gave it to the police?' he growled. 'Why? What made you go to the police?'

'They came to me,' she said as steadily as she could. 'A superintendent from Scotland Yard.'

'What did he want?' he demanded.

'He was inquiring into the murder of Mr. Haines,' she replied. She was going to add that the man known as Haines was really an escaped convict named Gilmore, but she decided that the less she said the better.

He uttered an oath, dropped her wrist, and began to pace up and down the room, frowning.

'You might as well let me go,' she said. 'You only wasted your time . . . '

'Did I? We'll see about that,' he snapped. He slipped his hand into his pocket and came over to her. Before she knew what he was going to do, he had seized her arm, taken something that glittered from his pocket, and she felt a sharp prick in her shoulder.

'That'll keep you quiet while I think,' he said.

She tried to scream in a sudden panic but her throat was suddenly constricted. She swayed, her knees gave away beneath her, and for the second time she lost consciousness . . .

★ ★ ★

Mr. Budd was a little disappointed when Janice Sheridan's maid gave him her mistress's message. He had brought round the photographs of John Gilmore, alias Jonathan Haines, in the hope that she might recognize them. The man had stated that he was a friend of her father's and it seemed likely that he had been speaking the truth. There appeared to be no other reason why he should have selected her for the guardian of the key otherwise.

After telling Alice that he would ring Miss Sheridan up later that day, or first thing on the following morning, he went back to the Yard with Hoppy, who had

124

accompanied him to the girl's flat.

When he reached his office, after leaving the reporter to go to Fleet Street, Mr. Budd found Leek poring over a sheet of paper with a stub of pencil in his hand. His long, thin face was contorted in an effort of concentration.

'So you've arrived at last, have you?' greeted the stout superintendent as he walked over to his desk. 'I thought I told you to get here at ten o'clock?'

Leek took no notice. His lips moved and he scrawled something on the paper in front of him.

Mr. Budd let himself down carefully into his chair.

'Did you hear what I was sayin'?' he inquired in a dangerously quiet voice. 'I was askin' why you're late?'

'I'm gaga, gaga, gaga,' muttered the lean sergeant, happily. 'That's it. I'm gaga, gaga, gaga . . .'

An expression of real alarm spread over Mr. Budd's fat face.

'Aren't you feelin' well?' he asked kindly.

'I'm gaga, gaga, gaga,' wailed Leek tunelessly. 'I'm gaga, gaga . . .'

'Listen here,' broke in Mr. Budd, 'just you sit quiet an' I'll get a doctor . . . '

Leek looked up in surprise. His fishlike eyes were vacant.

'What's that?' he asked, blankly. 'I never 'eard you come in . . . '

'Never mind,' interrupted the big man. 'You just keep quiet. I'll phone for a doctor.' He stretched out his hand toward the house phone.

'What do you want a doctor for?' asked Leek in astonishment. 'Aren't you well?'

'I'm all right,' replied Mr. Budd. 'It's you . . . '

'What's the matter with me?' asked Leek.

'You keep on sayin' you're gaga,' answered Mr. Budd. 'I asked you why you was late an' you said 'I'm gaga, gaga, gaga . . . '.'

'That's me new pop number,' explained the melancholy sergeant. 'I'm writin' it meself. It's rather good. Listen. 'I'm gaga, gaga, gaga, over you. Won't you be gaga, gaga, gaga over me? . . . ' 'I ain't got any further, but it's workin' up. Do you like it?'

Mr. Budd stared at him speechlessly. His face was a study. And then he took a deep breath.

'Do you mean to tell me that I've been wastin' my sympathy?' he snarled angrily. 'While you sit there scribblin' a lot o' trash . . . 'I'm gaga, gaga, gaga . . . ' Bah!'

'I think it's pretty good,' remarked Leek complacently. 'You wouldn't understand these things. You're a square . . . '

Mr. Budd controlled himself with an effort.

'I suppose you mean by that,' he said, 'that I like music that's got a tune to it an' isn't all alike, an' words that mean somethin', an' singers who can sing? If that's bein' a 'square', you're right. Now, you just forget all this rubbish, at least when you're supposed to be doin' your job.'

Leek sighed and folded up the scrap of paper he had been writing on and put it in his pocket.

'I'm sorry,' he said. 'Me enthusiasm was carryin' me away . . . '

'If it goes on,' said Mr. Budd darkly, 'it won't be enthusiasm that'll carry you away, me lad. It'll be the loony van an' you'll prob'ly find it packed with pop fans to keep you company.'

There came a tap at the door and a messenger entered. He handed Mr. Budd a filled in blank from the reception desk below.

The stout superintendent took it and glanced at it. He raised his eyebrows slightly.

'Send this feller up,' he said.

'Who's that?' asked Leek.

'It's the manager o' the pop singer's union,' replied Mr. Budd sarcastically. 'He's come to tell you that they're all goin' to work to rule unless you stick to bein' a sergeant in the C.I.D.'

The sergeant made a gesture of resignation.

'One o' these days,' he began and stopped as the door opened and a young man was shown in. He was a very good-looking and also a very agitated young man.

'Are you Superintendent Budd?' he demanded without preliminary.

'You're Mr. Crosse?' asked Mr. Budd sleepily.

'That's right,' said the young man. 'I've just come from Miss Janice Sheridan's flat. Her maid told me you'd an appointment with her this morning?'

'I did, but she had to go to the theatre . . . '

'That's just it,' broke in Crosse sharply. 'But she never got there and they never sent for her. A car called for her and she left in it, but she's disappeared.'

Mr. Budd sat up quickly and his face was grave.

8

It was quite a long time before Janice recovered consciousness for the second time. A racking pain was crawling to life in her tortured nerves and her head throbbed monotonously. She could feel every hammer-beat of her heart magnified a hundredfold, and her skin was hot and clammy and there was a feverish heat in her flesh that seemed to be burning her up. Subconsciously she knew that she was lying on something hard and lumpy, but she couldn't get up. Her numbed muscles refused to obey the signal from her brain. There seemed to be a kind of insulation between her and her senses.

Somewhere above her a blaze of light was stabbing at her eyes and hurting them. It cut into her head like hot knives and made her feel sick. Every now and again there was a queer feeling as though she were being rapidly revolved in a large drum with no chance of getting out or stopping the dizzy spinning. She closed her eyes and allowed herself to relax.

For a long time she lay, slipping back again into a state of dreamy lethargy. She was experiencing all the misery of the slow return to normality from the effects of the drug which had been injected into her system.

Presently she opened her eyes again. The light still blazed, white hot, above her, but now it did not seem so strong. It did not burn her eyes as it had done before. Vaguely she began to remember fragments of what had happened, and tried to disentangle them from the patches of vacancy that surrounded them. She got angry that she could not connect any of this jumbled mass of isolated glimpses into a coherent whole, and in the midst of her anger, drifted away again on a river of darkness . . .

When she woke again it was to full consciousness. She remembered every little detail that had happened to her, clearly and sharply. She was no longer in the room with the drawn curtains and the green shaded reading lamp. This room was smaller and more barely furnished. The walls were covered with a garish paper; the floor was bare without even a rug on the unstained boards. The thing she was lying on was an old horsehair sofa. This, with a plain table and a kitchen chair, was the only furniture.

From the centre of the dirty ceiling hung a single unshaded bulb. This gave all the light there was, for the only window had been heavily boarded up.

Janice, after one or two abortive attempts, got unsteadily off the sofa and looked about her.

Was this another room in the same house or had she been moved to some other place altogether? She looked for her wrist-watch and remembered that she had forgotten to put it on. She wondered if it was still day, but she had no means of telling. The air of the room was stuffy and smelt musty with that unpleasant smell that is associated with houses that have been long shut up and neglected.

Janice swallowed painfully. Her throat was dry and rough and she would have given almost anything for a cup of hot tea. She began to explore the room. The boards at the window were secured by rusty screws. The wood was thick and immovable. The door had been locked on the outside, as she discovered when she tried the handle. The room was as good as a prison. So far as she could see there was no possible means of getting out.

A sudden overwhelming feeling of panic swept over her, but she fought it down, and going back to the lumpy sofa, sat down to think. The exertion of walking about the room had tired her which showed that she was still weak from the drug.

She raised her head quickly as she heard a sound outside the door. It was the hollow sound of footsteps on bare boards. It stopped and there was a pause. Then there came a click as the key turned in the lock.

She stared at the door as it opened and the man she had seen before came in.

'You — you've come round,' he said. 'How are you feeling?'

He was carrying a writing-pad under his arm. He carefully locked the door behind him, crossed to the table and sat down.

'Where is this place?' she asked. 'This isn't the house you took me to before?'

'You are quite right,' he said. 'There's an old saying, 'exchange is no robbery'. I'm going to prove it's a true one.'

She looked at him in surprise.

'I want that key,' he continued. 'I'm willing to exchange you for it.'

'You must be mad,' she exclaimed.

'We shall see,' he retorted. 'You'd better hope that I'm right. Otherwise, you look like being here for a long time.'

'You can't keep me here,' she began but he interrupted her with an impatient gesture.

'Don't be silly,' he said curtly. 'I shall keep you as long as I like. Nobody knows where you are and I doubt if anyone would think of looking for you here.'

'Do you think that the police will give

up that key just so that I can go free?' she asked.

'I think so — under certain circumstances,' he replied. 'I want you to write to Scotland Yard.' He tapped the writing-pad which he had put down on the table. 'You will say that you are being kept a prisoner but that, so far, you are unhurt. How long you will remain so depends on how long it is before they hand over the key . . .'

'Do you imagine that they'll take any notice of that?' she said scornfully.

He nodded.

'Yes,' he answered. 'Particularly as you will add that for every day they delay in parting with the key, they will receive one of your fingers — just to remind them of the passing of time.'

Janice couldn't quite suppress the little gasp of horror that escaped her. The words had been quietly spoken but she knew that the man was quite capable of carrying out his threat.

'You wouldn't do it,' she whispered. 'You wouldn't dare do it.'

He shrugged his shoulders.

'I've no desire to be put to the test,' he said. 'Come over here and write the letter.'

He took a ball-pointed pen from his pocket and held it out to her.

'Write,' he ordered curtly.

She looked at him, saw the hard eyes full of an inflexible purpose, and got slowly to her feet . . .

* * *

It took a long time before Mr. Budd could get anything like coherence from the distracted young man. But at last he succeeded in getting the story from him.

'Come on,' said Mr. Budd, struggling to his feet. 'We'll go round to Miss Sheridan's flat.'

'What's the good of going there?' demanded Crosse. 'She isn't there, man, I tell you. She's gone . . . '

'I know, I know,' broke in Mr. Budd impatiently. 'But we've got to start somewhere an' that's the best place.' He signalled to Leek, and the lean sergeant followed them to the door.

A police car took them to Janice Sheridan's flat and they were admitted by the tearful Alice to the sitting-room. Mr. Budd questioned her, but the information she could supply was of the smallest.

She had caught only the vaguest glimpse of the man who had called for her mistress in the car. He had been wearing a chauffeur's uniform and she thought he had a little black moustache, but she wasn't sure of this. Her mistress had opened the door and she had only seen the man for a second as she came out of the sitting-room. She hadn't seen the car at all. Unless you leaned out of the window it was impossible to see a car if it was drawn up at the kerb, and she hadn't leaned out of the window. Why should she? She hadn't thought there was anything wrong.

Mr. Budd went down and interviewed the porter. But the porter had been out on a message and had seen nothing of the car, or the man who drove it.

There was a policeman on point duty a hundred yards down the road, and from him the stout superintendent succeeded in getting a description of the car. It was a large, black Buick saloon, of the kind that is usually let out for hire. The constable remembered that there was a glass partition between the passenger and the driver. The number was XY17 . . . something. The constable remembered the letters and the first two figures, but he couldn't remember the rest of it.

'I didn't think there was any call for me to take any particular notice, sir,' he said apologetically. 'But I'll take me oath on 'em being right.'

With this meagre information to work on, Mr. Budd went back to the Yard. From the Information Room an 'all stations' call went out with a description of Janice Sheridan and the car. There was a possible chance that this might have some result, though the stout superintendent was not very sanguine.

In less than an hour five thousand patrolling policemen would be on the look-out for the car in all parts of the country.

Mr. Budd felt that he had done all he

could for the moment. He had to use all his diplomacy to get rid of Jim Crosse who seemed to expect some kind of miraculous results from him, and was almost out of his mind with anxiety. Hoppy came up later in the afternoon and heard the news. He nearly wept when Mr. Budd refused to allow him to print a word of the story.

'Have a heart,' he entreated. 'This is news — big news! If any other paper gets hold of it, I'll be fired.'

'I don't want it in the papers yet,' snapped the big man. 'If nothin' is heard by this evenin' you can go ahead . . . '

'The people at the theatre will spill the beans,' groaned Hoppy. He stubbed out a Woodbine that he had just lighted and immediately lit another. 'This could be a scoop for the *Messenger* . . . '

'The theatre people 'ull say nothin',' promised Mr. Budd. 'I've been on to 'em an' told 'em to keep it quiet.'

'Can I wait in case something comes through?' pleaded the reporter, and Mr. Budd grudgingly agreed.

For the remainder of the afternoon

they waited, but there was nothing. The girl had vanished into thin air.

Mr. Budd had no illusions concerning the reason for her disappearance. It didn't require a great deal of thought to put his finger on that reason. She had been kidnapped because of the key. That was quite obviously at the bottom of it.

But what would the unknown murderer do when he discovered that it was no longer in her possession? Would he let her go? The stout superintendent thought that it was very unlikely. She would of course, tell her captor that the key was in the hands of the police. He would try to use her as a bargaining asset.

If he were right there was no particular reason to worry about the girl. She would be quite safe until this man had put forward his proposal, what-ever-it-was.

He tried to explain this to Jim Crosse, who kept on ringing up for news, but the young man was inconsolable. He wanted action, and nearly drove the big man to distraction with his insistence.

The day came to an end without any

news, and Hoppy, having got through an incredible number of his inevitable Woodbines, raced down to Fleet Street with the news when Mr. Budd, true to his promise, lifted his ban.

The *Messenger* carried a front page story about Janice Sheridan's abduction on the following morning and it was the only newspaper with the story. Hoppy had got his scoop to the delight of his news editor.

When Mr. Budd arrived at the Yard, there was news at last. A patrolling policeman at Putney had found an A.A. man who had seen a car, answering to the description of the black Buick, at the junction of Putney Hill and the Portsmouth Road at a little after six on the previous evening.

'I think it was the car you want, sir,' said the messenger from the Information Room, 'The constable says that the A.A. man noticed a girl in the back who looked ill.'

'Did you get the direction the car was goin'?' asked Mr. Budd.

'It turned off in the direction of

Wimbledon, sir,' answered the man. He was a little annoyed when it seemed that the stout superintendent wasn't even listening. He had opened one of the letters that lay on his desk and was frowning at it.

'I think this is more important,' he murmured. 'All right, Smithson. Thanks for the information.'

The messenger departed, and Mr. Budd returned to his perusal of the letter in his podgy hand. It was written on cheap paper and ran as follows:

Dear Superintendent Budd,

I am being forced to write this. I don't know where I am but I am being kept prisoner. I am quite safe but how long I shall be rests with the police. If you will give up the key which I gave you, I shall be set free. A car with a red light on the left-hand mudguard will be waiting at twelve o'clock tonight along the portion of the Portsmouth Road that runs beside Wimbledon Common. Give the driver the key. If you don't I shall lose a finger for every time that

the messenger returns without the key.
If you try to detain or follow the
messenger I shall be killed. Please do
what I ask.

Janice Sheridan.

Leek came in as Mr. Budd finished reading the letter for the third time.

'Any news?' asked the lean sergeant, and Mr. Budd gave him the letter.

'What are you goin' ter do?' asked Leek, when he had read it.

'What can we do?' said Mr. Budd, shrugging his broad shoulders. 'We daren't ignore this and risk that girl bein' maimed. I s'pose I shall have to keep this appointment.'

'D'you want me to go with you?' inquired Leek.

Mr. Budd shook his head.

'Not with me,' he said. 'Ahead of me. You can take Harkness with you. You'd better get there early an' find a place where you can watch for the arrival of this car. But you'd better make sure that you're not spotted — for the girl's sake. You'll follow the car *after* I've given this feller the key. Harkness had best use his motor-cycle, but for Pete's sake take care. I may have to part with this key, but I'm expectin' to get it back, and with it the murderer!'

9

Janice woke from a fitful sleep and found that during her short sleep somebody had entered the room and left a tray on the table.

The sight of it made her realise just how hungry she was. She lifted the newspaper which covered the tray and found a plate of sandwiches and a bottle of milk.

She ate the sandwiches ravenously and drank the milk, feeling better for the nourishment. Her captor evidently had no intention of starving her, at any rate.

She wondered if the letter he had forced her to write would have any effect. Would the superintendent ignore it? Even if he didn't, would the man who was holding her in this place keep his word?

Once he had got the key there was no reason why he should let her go. In fact, it was dangerous. It would be to his advantage to kill her — as he had already killed Gilmore. It would be so easy. No one knew where she was. He could kill her and dump her body on some lonely road in the country and nobody would be able to find him.

The idea grew in her mind until she shivered at the picture her imagination conjured up.

The more she thought about it the more depressed she became. Half this state of mind was due to the drug that had been administered to her, but she didn't realize this. She didn't even know what time it was, or whether it was day or night. She had no idea how long she had slept. She rose in a sudden panic and began to pace up and down the room. Presently the purely physical movement soothed her ragged nerves. She grew a little calmer, and racked her brains for some means of escape.

If only she could get away — away from this horrible room with its flamboyant paper and its musty odour. Was there any way of opening the door? She had already examined the window and decided that

that was impossible. Without a screw-driver, or something like it, it would be impossible to shift the screws that held the boards in position.

She went over to the door and tried the handle for the tenth time. It was no good. The door was solid and the lock was a stout one . . .

She went suddenly rigid. The faint creak of a footfall reached her. The man was coming back!

She looked about her wildly and was struck by a brilliant idea. So simple that it took her breath away! She was at the table in two silent strides and picked up the empty milk bottle. As silently she was back at the door with the bottle in her hand. Crouching back against the wall by the side of the door, she waited.

The footsteps had stopped, and she held her breath. But they came on again and, with her heart beating wildly, she waited, the bottle raised above her head.

There was a soft click of a turning key in the lock, the door swung open, and the man came in. He stopped when he couldn't see her. He took another step forward and Janice brought the milk bottle down with all her force on his head.

The blow was a heavy one. He gave a gasping grunt and fell on his knees. For a second she looked down at him as he slumped sideways and sprawled at her feet. The room was spinning about her and she felt faint, but she pulled herself together and stepped quickly through the open door.

She was free!

She was in a narrow passage that led to a landing. There was no sound anywhere and she crept forward toward a dim light that shone from somewhere below. She concluded it came from the hall. Reaching the landing, she came to the head of a narrow staircase leading downwards. Beneath was a small and very dirty hall, unfurnished completely. On a nail in the wall hung a man's overcoat and hat. The light came from a dust-encrusted bulb that hung from the cracked ceiling.

She ran down the staircase and as she did so she heard a scrabbling sound from above. The man had recovered his senses. Heavy breathing was followed by staggering steps.

'Where are you?' he shouted thickly. 'Come back . . . '

Although her head ached so badly she could hardly see, she felt her way across the hall and fumbled with the fastenings of the front door. Her fingers trembled so much that she could scarcely pull back the bolts, but she succeeded at last and turned the catch of the patent lock. To her dismay the door only opened a few inches and she saw that the chain was on.

Blundering footsteps were coming down the stairs. In a panic she wrenched at the chain, glancing back over her shoulder.

The man was coming down the stairs clutching at the banister rail as he swayed from stair to stair. He saw her and gave a hoarse shout.

But she had managed to get the chain free and fling open the door. She stumbled out into the cool, fresh air. It was quite dark and the rain was falling. A short flight of steps led down to a gravel path. Again she heard a shout behind her, and running down the steps she made off as fast as she could along the gravel path. The unsteady sound of footsteps came after her. She flew along a dark path lined by bushes, the branches of which tore at her clothes and scratched her face. She had no idea where she was going, but she ran as hard as she could. The path took a sudden turn and she almost fell into a closed gate. She tugged at it and, to her joy, it opened easily. There was a road beyond the gate and down this she sped, the footsteps of her pursuer stumbling along behind her. The narrow road frayed away into uneven grassland. She found herself in the middle of thinly growing trees which got thicker and closer as she went on. There was sharp pain in her side and flashes of light danced before her eyes. Her feet felt as if they were shod with lead. But fear forced her on and on, although she was stumbling now, and twice she nearly fell.

She came out from the shelter of the trees into a clearing, tripped over the root of a tree, fell heavily and struck her head on a stone . . .

She came to, cold and shivering, and somebody was saying in a gruff voice: 'Here what's all this? What's the matter here?'

A man was bending over her, shining the light of an electric lantern in her face. She started up with a cry, and then she saw the shining black of the wet cape and fell back with a gasp of relief as she saw that the man who held the lamp was a policeman.

'Where am I?' she asked with difficulty.

'Wimbledon Common,' he answered suspiciously. 'What's the matter, miss? How did you get here?'

Janice sat up and pressed a hand to her aching head.

'I fell and hurt myself,' she answered faintly. 'Could you — could you get me a taxi?'

The constable looked at her doubtfully.

'I'd like to know a bit more about this, miss,' he said. 'Where did you come from?'

Disjointedly, Janice began to tell him, but she only got as far as her name when he interrupted her.

'Gosh!' he exclaimed. 'You're the lady we've all been looking for! You'd better come with me to the station, miss.'

'I'd rather go home,' she said. 'I'm very cold and tired.'

'We'll see you get home as soon as possible,' promised the constable, 'but I'm afraid you'll have to come to the station first, miss. It's not far.'

He helped her to her feet, and, supporting her with his arm, led her to the main road.

The Inspector in charge of the police station listened to her story, put one or two questions, and then arranged for a police car to take her home to her flat.

A delighted and surprised Alice was awakened and insisted on preparing a meal. After she had eaten it and had two cups of tea, Janice went to bed and fell almost instantly asleep.

* * *

Mr. Budd, uncomfortably wedged in a chair that was much too small for his bulk, looked sleepily at the girl who was sitting up in bed, nibbling toast.

The stout superintendent had learned that the girl had been found when he returned to the Yard after he had been to keep his appointment with the unknown at twelve o'clock. No car with a red light on the wing had come. Mr. Budd, after waiting for an hour, had gone back to the Yard a very disappointed man, to hear that Janice had been found on Wimbledon Common and was now in bed and asleep. As early as possible on the following morning, he called at the girl's flat to hear her story, part of which had already been relayed from the police station by the inspector in charge. He knew, now, why the murderer had not come for the key.

'It was a horrible experience,' said Janice, sipping orange juice. 'Do you think you'll be able to find that house?'

'I don't think it'll be difficult, miss,'

said the big man. 'Sergeant Leek has gone along to make some inquiries. Whether it's goin' to help us much, I couldn't say. This feller who kept you prisoner knows that you've got away, an' he'll realize that you've told the police. You can bet that 'e won't hang around.'

She shivered slightly.

'I suppose the man was the same person who murdered Gilmore?' she said.

'Oh, yes, there's no doubt about that, miss,' said Mr. Budd. 'And Phyllida Loveridge an' Maitland.' He shook his head sadly. 'I slipped up there, you know. When you told me about the key I should've had you watched. I might have caught this feller, if I had.'

'Who is he?' she asked.

Mr. Budd slowly shook his head.

'I don't know, miss,' he answered. 'Have you any idea at all where you were taken to first?'

'Not the slightest,' she replied. 'The room was very well furnished. It was nothing like the other house.'

'What about the man?' went on the stout superintendent. 'Can you remember anythin' about him that might help us?'

She frowned and hesitated.

'I'm not sure,' she said. 'It seemed that I'd met him somewhere before . . . '

Mr. Budd leaned forward. His sleepy-looking eyes were very wide open.

'Try an' think, miss,' he urged. 'It might be important. What was it that made you think you'd met this feller somewhere before?'

'It was something in his voice,' she answered reluctantly. 'It reminded me of a — a great friend of my father's . . . '

'What was his name?' asked Mr. Budd.

'Walter Renfrew,' she said. She paused. 'I think I'd better tell you the whole story,' she went on. 'You see, my mother married again — a year after my father died. She married the man who had been his greatest friend . . . '

'Renfrew?' put in the stout superintendent.

She nodded.

'Yes. It was not a happy marriage. He took all the money she had — an aunt left her a large legacy after my father died — and a year later Walter Renfrew deserted her. My mother died soon afterwards.'

'Have you any idea where he is now?'

'No. He disappeared completely after he left mother.'

'And was this feller at all like Renfrew?'

'Not in the least.'

'Only somethin' in his voice reminded you?'

She nodded.

'What was Renfrew like, miss? You haven't a photograph?'

'No. I'll try and describe him. He was tall and very good-looking. He had fair hair and blue eyes . . . '

'Any distinguishin' marks? A scar or anythin' of the kind?'

'I believe that he suffered from a fractured knee-cap. I remember father mentioning that the doctor had never attended to it properly at the time, and it had left Renfrew slightly lame.'

'In the left leg,' murmured Mr. Budd softly.

Janice looked surprised.

'How did you know that?' she asked.

Mr. Budd made no reply to this.

Instead he asked another question.

'How did your father die, miss?'

'He was run over,' she answered. 'He was away on a short holiday with Walter Renfrew . . . ' She stopped and into her eyes came a look of horror. 'Oh . . . You don't think . . . '

'Not yet,' interrupted Mr. Budd. 'I'm just gatherin' information, miss. I might start thinkin' later.'

She looked at him steadily.

'I see,' she said. 'Well, I'll tell you anything I can.'

'Thank you, miss,' said the big man gratefully. 'Was your mother with your father when the accident happened?'

'No. It was Walter Renfrew who broke the news to her, four days after it happened.'

'Four days?' said Mr. Budd. 'What was the reason for the delay?'

'It was rather a thoughtful one, according to what my mother told me. Father was so badly wounded — a heavy lorry went over his head — that Renfrew didn't want my mother to see him. He made all the arrangements for the funeral before he told her.'

'Did your mother attend the funeral?'

'She was too ill. The shock of hearing about father's death brought on a breakdown. She was never very strong.'

'An' a year after she married Walter Renfrew?'

'Yes.'

'How long ago did this happen, miss?' asked Mr. Budd.

'Let me see — it would be about eight years ago,' she answered after a little thought.

Mr. Budd nodded. He put his hand in his breast pocket and produced an envelope. From the envelope he took out two photographs.

'Do you recognise those, miss,' he asked gently.

Janice took the photographs. One glance she gave at them and gasped.

'Where did you get these?' she demanded.

'Do you recognise the man in those photographs?' said Mr. Budd.

'Yes,' she replied huskily. 'They're photographs of my father . . . '

'They're also photographs of John Gilmore, alias Jonathan Haines, who was murdered in his house at Barnet,' said Mr. Budd quietly.

10

Mr. Budd was not surprised. It couldn't be said that he expected to hear that Gilmore and Janice's father were one and the same, but he was not surprised. It was just something to add to his list of facts from which he could weave a theory that would lead him to the truth.

Jim Crosse arrived almost at the same moment, a delighted and surprised young man, and the stout superintendent discreetly took his leave.

Leek had just come back, when he reached the Yard, with a report about the house at Wimbledon.

It was an empty house on the outskirts of the common, or rather it was partly empty, for the previous tenants had left behind one or two sticks of furniture. A visit to the estate agents who had the letting of the house had resulted in precisely nothing. The man who had used it had had no authority from them. How he had got hold of the key they couldn't imagine.'

'I can,' grunted Mr. Budd. 'All he had to do was to get an order to view an' take an impression. It'd've been easy. Go on.'

'That's about all there is,' said the lean sergeant. 'We searched the house but there wasn't anythin'. The feller got away in a car. You could see the tyre marks in the wet gravel.'

'Did you get a list o' the people who'd had orders to view recently?' asked the big man and Leek nodded.

'There was only one an' 'e was an old man,' said the sergeant.

'I'll bet he was,' remarked Mr. Budd, sceptically.

'I've put me name down for the police concert at Wimbledon,' said Leek. 'I'm goin' to sing.'

'Heaven help 'em!' exclaimed Mr. Budd. 'I oughter warn 'em. They don't know what to expect . . . '

'The local inspector asked me,' explained the sergeant.

'He *asked* you?' repeated the big man. 'How did he know you could do anythin' to 'elp at a concert?'

'Well, I let drop that I was a pop singer in me spare time,' said Leek. 'He jumped at me.'

'He'll jump *on* you when he knows what you've let him in for,' growled Mr. Budd. 'You oughter be locked up. You're a danger to the public.'

'You'll feel different after you've 'eard me,' said Leek.

'Are you seriously expectin' that I'm coming to hear you caterwaulin'? Pop singer! You'd do better as Popeye.'

'You don't have to be rude,' complained the injured Leek. 'Anybody who's got a hidden talent . . . '

'Your talent is so well hidden,' snarled Mr. Budd, 'that it'd take a bulldozer to dig it out!'

Leek reddened. He opened his mouth to reply when Hoppy came breezing into the office.

'Hello, hello,' he greeted. 'Well, you're a pal, you are! Why didn't you let me know that Janice Sheridan was back?'

'How *did* you know?' demanded the stout superintendent.

'I rang up her flat to ask the maid a question,' said Hoppy with a grin. He took out his inevitable packet of Woodbines and lit one. 'What's fresh? Any other news?'

'Not for publication,' said Mr. Budd.

'That means there is,' broke in Hoppy. 'Come on — spill it.'

Mr. Budd told him what he had learned that morning from Janice.

Hoppy whistled.

'Well, well,' he said. 'Never a dull moment, eh? So the dead man was Janice Sheridan's father.'

'Apparently,' murmured Mr. Budd.

'I suppose she is quite *sure*?' said the reporter. 'It couldn't be a chance resemblance?'

'I think she's sure enough,' said the big man. 'That means that the man who was run over wasn't Gilmore, or Sheridan to give him his real name.'

'My dear Holmes, you surprise me!' grinned Hoppy.

'You just cut out tryin' to be funny an' listen,' retorted Mr. Budd. 'What I'm gettin' at is this. This feller Renfrew

163

must've known that the man who was killed wasn't Sheridan. He was with him when it happened an' he got him all nicely buried an' safely out of the way before anyone could have a chance of spottin' that the dead man *wasn't* Sheridan.'

'It must have been with the connivance of Sheridan himself,' put in Hoppy. 'Why should he let Renfrew pass him off for dead when he wasn't? And why should Renfrew want to? What motive had he?'

'Don't get so impatient,' said the stout superintendent. 'I don't know yet. I'm just sort o' tryin' to figure things out . . . '

'There doesn't seem to be much doubt that Renfrew is the man who killed Sheridan an' the others,' put in the reporter. 'But I can't see what his motive was, or why he is so anxious to get hold of this key.'

'The key is tied up with this play that Sheridan wrote,' answered Mr. Budd, 'an' which the murderer — we won't call him Renfrew yet — was so anxious nobody should see. Now, accordin' to Mrs.

164

Bishop, this play had somethin' to do with a murder . . . '

'The murder of Joseph Wurtz?' interrupted Hoppy. Mr. Budd nodded.

'We can take that as a basis to work on,' he agreed. 'Sheridan, in the name of John Gilmore, was arrested for the killin' of the moneylender, but he swore at the time that he was innocent. He made a statement which he said was what had actually happened. It seemed a pretty weak kind of story, but it could've been true. Supposin' it *was* true . . . ?'

'You mean,' said Hoppy, 'that he discovered some proof of his story after he escaped from prison and wrote this play . . . ?' He stopped and shook his head. 'It's absurd. Why didn't he go straight to the police and tell them? If he had sufficient proof of his innocence they'd have done something about it, wouldn't they? Why adopt such a fanciful idea as writing a play about it?'

'Unless you can understand the full truth,' said the big man, 'I'll agree that it does sound a bit silly. But, maybe, Sheridan had his reasons. I've an idea

165

that the key would tell us all we want to know . . . '

'If we could find the lock it fits,' said Hoppy.

'We will,' answered Mr. Budd. 'It may take time but we'll find the lock.' He sighed. 'It's a complicated business. I don't think I've ever had to deal with a more complicated case, but it'll all come out in the wash.'

'What's your next move?' asked the reporter. 'It seems to have reached a bit of a deadlock.'

'It's a question of time,' said Mr. Budd sleepily. 'I've got to go into that very carefully.'

'Time?' Hoppy looked surprised. 'You mean before this man manages to get away?'

'I don't mean anythin' of the kind,' grunted Mr. Budd. 'I'm not talkin' about that sort o' time. I'm talkin' about dates. They might prove to be very interestin'.'

He hoisted himself out of his chair with a prodigious yawn.

'You'd better clear out now,' he said. 'I've got a lot of investigatin' to do . . . '

Hoppy took the hint. 'All right,' he said cheerfully. 'I'll pop in again later . . . '

'Much later,' said Mr. Budd.

When the reporter had gone, he went over and struggled into his overcoat.

'Will yer want me?' ventured Leek. 'I'm feelin' a bit tired . . . '

'When d'you feel anythin' else?' remarked the big man scathingly. 'You was born tired.'

'I didn't get much sleep last night,' explained the sergeant, 'an' I was out early this mornin' . . . '

'All right,' grunted Mr. Budd. 'You can hop off for a couple of hours an' dream yourself silly! Not that you have to dream much for that!' he added darkly. 'But don't be longer than two hours. I may have a job for you when I come back.'

'What job?' asked the sergeant unhappily.

'I'm not sure yet,' replied Mr. Budd. 'You'll know when I've made up me mind.'

He left the Yard and made his way to the little teashop in Whitehall where he did a great deal of his thinking and pondering. Ordering a pot of tea and two rounds of buttered toast, he sat himself down at a table in the corner and began to cogitate.

There was this question of dates to be cleared up. Janice Sheridan had stated that her father had 'died' about eight years ago while he was on a short holiday with Walter Renfrew. But this didn't make sense with the date that Wurtz had been killed. That had been eight years ago, too. Sheridan, alias Gilmore, alias Haines, couldn't have been in two places at once. He couldn't have been on holiday with Renfrew and being arrested for murder at the same time.

This raised the question of the identity of the man who *had* been killed. Somebody had definitely been run over by a lorry and buried in the name of Sheridan. Who was this man?

Mr. Budd had taken the trouble to ring up Janice and find out where Renfrew and Sheridan had been on holiday when the supposed death of Sheridan had taken place.

It was a small village in Devonshire.

The stout superintendent considered that inquiries would have to be made there so that he could obtain the full details of what had actually happened. It was a long time ago but there should be someone who would remember. This unknown man who had died, and whom Renfrew had passed off as Sheridan — why hadn't he been missed? Surely someone must have wondered what had happened to him?

There was another thing. Had Sheridan been a party to the deception, or had Renfrew been solely responsible? If Sheridan had been in it, why had he allowed it? It couldn't have had anything to do with the murder of Wurtz because that must have come later. Even if it hadn't been much later. So what motive could Sheridan have for wishing his family to believe that he was dead?

Or what motive had Renfrew, if he had carried out the deception on his own?

Mr. Budd sighed, gulped a cup of tea, and munched some of his toast. It was, as he had said, very complicated.

Another thing that wanted clearing up

was the letter that should have reached Janice after her father's death — his real death this time — explaining the key.

No sign of any letter had, as yet, turned up. There was time, of course. Wherever the letter was coming from, whoever was holding it for delivery to Janice, must have known Sheridan in his assumed name of Haines. That seemed fairly obvious, because if Sheridan had taken precautions to ensure that his daughter should receive this letter after his death, it must have been in the name of Jonathan Haines. It would be 'Jonathan Haines' who would die.

Did this letter actually exist? Or had Sheridan *intended* to write such a letter and arrange for its delivery and been killed before he had been able to do so?

That was possible, though it seemed almost incredible that he would have neglected this important part of his plan whatever-it-was. If the letter was in existence, who had it? A solicitor was the most likely. But why hadn't this solicitor carried out his instructions? He must have been aware of 'Jonathan

Haines's' murder. The newspapers had been full of it. He would either have communicated with the police or with Janice Sheridan . . . So why hadn't he?

Mr. Budd finished his toast and drained the teapot of its last drop of tea. Producing a notebook from his pocket, he jotted down one or two notes. He finished with two items that struck him as requiring attention:

1. *Was Sheridan a rich man? Had he been in any kind of business?*
2. *What had happened to his money after his supposed death? Had it gone to his widow?*

'Jonathan Haines' had apparently had plenty of money. He had taken the house in Barnet, and he had furnished it expensively. Where had this come from? 'Gilmore' — all these names, thought the stout superintendent, were a bit confusing — couldn't have had any money when he escaped from prison, but he had evidently known where to get it. Where *had* he got it?

Mr. Budd paid his bill and left the little teashop. He had not exaggerated when he had told Hoppy that he had a lot of investigating to do . . .

* * *

When Leek returned to the Yard, he found Mr. Budd seated at his desk consulting a slip of paper with some scribbled figures on it, his brows drawn down and his thick lips pursed. He looked up as the lean sergeant came reluctantly into the cheerless office.

'Here you are, are you?' grunted the stout superintendent. 'I hope you've had a good rest 'cos you've got a journey before you.'

'Where am I goin'?' asked Leek dismally.

'You're goin' down to a village in Devon called Torbridge,' answered Mr. Budd. 'I've been on to the p'lice at the nearest town an' they'll give you any help you want . . . '

'What am I goin' to do when I get there?' inquired Leek in dismay. He

172

hadn't a great deal of enthusiasm for this unexpected journey. 'What's the idea?'

'Mine,' said Mr. Budd. 'An' if you keep quiet for a minute, I'll tell you what you've got to do.'

Leek sat down in the only other available chair.

'I want you to find out,' continued Mr. Budd, 'all you can about an accident that happened in Torbridge eight years ago. A man was run over by a lorry an' killed.'

'I dig you,' said the sergeant brightly.

'What the hell d'you mean by that?' demanded the big man.

'I mean I understand what you're sayin',' explained the sergeant.

'Then why can't you say so in plain English?' snarled Mr. Budd. ' 'I dig you'. Good Lord, what are we comin' to? This feller was supposed to be Sheridan, got that?'

Leek nodded. He thought it was safer than saying anything.

'But,' went on the big man, 'of course, he wasn't Sheridan because, accordin' to the dates I've got here, at the time of the accident, Sheridan, in the name of John

Gilmore was already under arrest for the murder of Wurtz . . . '

'Then who was this chap who was run over?' asked Leek.

'That's what you're goin' to Torbridge to find out,' replied Mr. Budd. 'The p'lice haven't any record of anybody bein' reported as missin' at that time, but there *was* a man run over, an' somebody must know who he was. Somebody must've missed this feller. I want to know who he was . . . '

'It ain't goin' to be easy after eight years,' complained the sergeant. 'How'm I goin' to start?'

'By gettin' on a train for Devonshire,' retorted Mr. Budd. 'After you get to Torbridge, it's up to you. Now, here's the time of the next train, get goin'.'

Sergeant Leek took the slip his superior pushed across the desk to him and looked at it. His long face brightened a little as he saw that the time of the next train would give him over two hours to prepare for the journey.

'Don't go singin' to anybody,' warned Mr. Budd as Leek was leaving the office.

'We don't want to give the Devonshire people a bad impression of Scotland Yard.'

'I'll be seein' you,' said the sergeant.

He had no idea as he said it under what circumstances he was to see Mr. Budd again.

11

The man in the large room with the green-shaded reading lamp on the writing-table, paced up and down restlessly. Janice Sheridan would have recognized him for the man in the chauffeur's uniform who had come to take her to the theatre and had brought her to this room instead.

But his appearance was not his own.

The disguise was slight but efficient. It completely altered him. The colour of the hair was different to his own; his complexion was swarthy instead of fair; the small moustache had been carefully put on, until it looked entirely natural. Even the shape of his nose had been slightly changed by the skilful use of wax. There was no make-up in the sense that an actor uses it. This was more subtle; relying on small detail; a tiny alteration to the line of the eyebrows; a difference in the way the hair was brushed.

He looked worried. The key! That was

the one thing left that could prove his undoing. The manuscript and both the typescripts of the play had been destroyed. He had acted quickly and guarded against that danger.

But the key! That was the greatest danger of all!

And he knew where it was. He only had to get it. But that wasn't so easy. If only that damned girl hadn't escaped . . .

He stopped at a small table and poured himself out a John Haig. His hands were shaking and he felt in need of something to steady his nerves. Gulping down the neat spirit, he resumed his ceaseless promenade of the room.

Until he had that key in his possession he could never feel safe. He cursed the man who had taken this means of revenging himself. Up to the moment when he had discovered the real identity of 'Jonathan Haines' life had been smooth and pleasant. There was nothing to fear.

Well, he had dealt satisfactorily with *that*. He paused and wiped his forehead as he remembered that feverish night of activity. He had had to work fast. There was no time to waste, scarcely time to think. He had carried out what had to be done successfully. He had secured all the evidence against himself and destroyed it . . .

Except the key . . .

There must be a way to deal with that if only he could think of it.

He poured himself another stiff whisky, carried it over to an easy chair, sat down and concentrated on his urgent problem . . .

* * *

Mr. Budd let himself into his little villa at Streatham with his latch-key. He was looking forward to an evening with a new book on the growing of roses, which was his hobby. This was a book that had only recently been published and contained a lot of fresh information on the subject. The stout superintendent loved roses. His small garden was aflame with bloom, and drenched in perfume, throughout the summer and long into the autumn. This was one of the few things of which his dour housekeeper fully approved. She had been as pleased as Mr. Budd himself when the big man had won both first and second prizes in the local rose show.

He had finished his dinner and settled himself with the book in an easy chair in front of the electric fire, when the front door bell rang.

Mr. Budd frowned. He wasn't expecting anybody. If there had been any important news from the Yard they would have telephoned. He had done all he could do, at the moment, on the Barnet case before he left, and the inquiry that he had set in motion would be a long and tedious investigation from which there couldn't possibly be any results as quickly as this.

The bell rang again and he laid down his book, and was hoisting himself out of his chair, when he heard the housekeeper, muttering to herself, pass along the passage to the hall. He heard the front door opened and a murmur of voices, and then the housekeeper tapped on the door of the sitting-room and thrust her head in.

'There's a boy with a note,' she said. 'He's waiting for an answer.'

Mr. Budd sighed, got up, and took the envelope she held out through the partly open door. Tearing it open he scanned the contents.

'I have just remembered something about the man who held me prisoner that might help you to identify him. Can you come and see me at the theatre tonight? I think it is important and urgent.

Janice Sheridan.'

Now long experience had made Mr. Budd a cautious and suspicious man. The note might be genuine, but on the other hand it might not. How, for instance, had Janice Sheridan known his private address?

'Keep that boy for a moment,' he said in a low voice to his housekeeper. 'Tell him I'll be out in a minute.'

She nodded and withdrew her head.

Mr. Budd stepped quickly over to the telephone that stood on a corner table, quickly found the number of the Majestic Theatre, and dialled it. There was a little delay, during which he could hear the housekeeper arguing with the messenger, and then he was through to the stage doorkeeper. He put his question. Janice Sheridan was on the stage and not available. The big man drew in his breath in exasperation. He couldn't keep the boy waiting for long. If the note was a fake, as he suspected, he would grow suspicious.

He hung up the receiver and thought quickly. There was only one thing to do. He would have to pretend that he was going to the theatre.

He went out into the hall. His housekeeper was holding a rather shabbily-dressed youth by the arm, whose unprepossessing face wore a look of alarm.

'Wasn't going to wait,' she said curtly. 'But I soon fixed that.'

'You let me go,' broke in the youth angrily. 'Wotcher think you're doin', eh?'

'It's all right, me lad,' interposed Mr. Budd. 'Did you bring this note from the theatre?'

'That's right,' said the youth.

'How did you get here?' went on the big man.

'Come by bus,' answered the other.

'I see,' said Mr. Budd genially. 'Well, you can come back with me in my car.'

The youth looked disconcerted.

'I was give me return fare,' he said.

Mr. Budd was now quite sure that the whole thing was a fake. This was another attempt to get hold of the key. He wasn't sure what the unknown murderer had in mind, but he was quite certain that the note had nothing to do with Janice Sheridan. The fact that her name had been used showed clearly who it had come from.

The stout superintendent's brain worked quickly. If he detained this boy it would probably do little or no good. He had merely been picked somewhere for the job, told what to say and do, and that was all. But there was the possibility that, if Mr. Budd handled it properly, the youth might lead him to the man who had sent him.

'P'raps you'd better go back the way

you came,' said the big man after a pause. 'I shan't be ready to go yet. Are you goin' back to Miss Sheridan?'

The youth nodded.

'Well, you tell her,' said Mr. Budd untruthfully, 'that as soon as I've had a meal, I'll come an' see her.'

'Right yer are, gov'nor,' exclaimed the youth with obvious relief. 'I'll cut along . . .'

He turned quickly and scuttled out the front door. Mr. Budd seized his hat from the stand, jerked down his overcoat, and pulling it on as he went, hurried through to the kitchen and out the back door. He moved with a speed and agility that was incredible in so stout a man. A path led round to the front, and he reached the gate in time to see the youth slouching down the road.

Mr. Budd crossed the street and followed on the other side. The youth looked back twice, but the stout superintendent was an expert on the art of trailing a quarry, and the boy saw nothing to rouse his suspicions.

Near the end of the street there was a

car drawn up at the kerb. Mr. Budd could see the dim lights. He guessed that the youth was making for this car. It was a flash of that inspiration that sometimes stood him in such good stead. He increased his pace until he had passed the youth on the other side of the road.

He moved silently, like a shadow, and before the boy had reached the car, Mr. Budd had almost got to the end of the street and crossed over to the pavement where the car waited.

He hadn't been mistaken. It was a large black saloon. He could make out the registration number: XY1703. The XY 17 . . . that the constable had remembered.

Mr. Budd moved into the shadow of a gateway. In that car lurked the murderer — almost within his reach!

He watched the boy draw level with the car and stop. He tapped on the window and, leaning forward, peered into the driving seat . . .

It may have been that Mr. Budd was so intent on watching the youth that his usual alertness was dulled. He only heard the faint sound behind him when it was too late. Something was suddenly thrown over his head and he inhaled the sickly fumes of chloroform with which it was soaked. He struggled to free his head from the enveloping cloth, but his senses were reeling . . .

He was forced forward, his struggles growing more feeble as the drug took a more powerful grip . . .

And then — blackness!

* * *

Mr. Budd opened his eyes to the accompaniment of an agonizing pain in his head. It was the worst headache he had ever experienced. He felt a sickness in the pit of his stomach, and became dimly aware of a curious swaying motion. His half-conscious mind associated this vaguely with the sea. What was he doing on the sea? The darkness came down again like a dropped curtain and he felt himself apparently floating away on soft and undulating clouds . . .

Once more the dark curtain lifted, but he was still only in semi-possession of his normal senses. What on earth was happening to him?

Slowly, little by little, the fumes of the chloroform began to wear off. His brain cleared, and recollection came back to him.

He remembered the youth who had called with the note; remembered following him and seeing the car; remembered crossing the road and taking up his position in the gateway.

What had happened there?

Something had been thrown over his head — a heavy, blanket-like cloth . . . He remembered the sickly smell of the chloroform with which the cloth had been soaked, and his struggling against the overpowering drug . . . And that was all.

Where was he now? The cloth was apparently still round his head for he could see nothing at all, only blackness. He tried to raise his hands to tear off the cloth, but he couldn't. His arms had been strapped or bound to his sides and further movement told him that his legs had been treated in a similar manner.

He was quite helpless.

Mr. Budd lay still and thought. He had succeeded in placing the curious swaying motion that had made him think of the sea. He could feel the vibration and hear the swish of wheels. He was in a car — probably the black saloon that had been standing by the kerb.

The stout superintendent muttered derogatory remarks about himself. He had been caught like the veriest tyro.

Well, it wasn't much use crying over spilt milk. The murderer had proved smarter than he. And he wasn't in a very enviable position. The man who had trapped him was quite ruthless. He would stick at nothing to get what he wanted.

And, of course, what he wanted was the key.

Mr. Budd started to work his head about to try and free it from the cloth. It couldn't have been the same cloth because there was no smell of chloroform to this one. At last, with much difficulty, and by rubbing the cloth against the cushioned back of the seat on which he lay, he was able to disentangle himself from the material.

The movement caused his head to throb violently and he had to lie still for a few minutes to ease the pain. It abated a little after a while and he cautiously raised his head. He soon found that the absence of the cloth had made practically no difference to his being able to see anything, for the blinds at the windows were down, and the darkness was still intense. He could dimly make out through the glass in front, however, the shadowy figure of the driver silhouetted against the faint light from the sky. They seemed to be travelling at a pretty fair speed, but where they were going he hadn't an idea.

Well, that wasn't very important. The thing that *was* important was how he could turn the tables on his captor. If the unknown man was expecting to get the key, he was due for a big disappointment. And that wouldn't make him too good tempered!

Mr. Budd thought there might be a spot of trouble — very unpleasant trouble. He would have to use his brains to get out of it, and he sincerely hoped that they wouldn't let him down.

The sudden slowing of the car, and a sharp turn to the right, made him suddenly alert. He thought, now that his eyes were getting more accustomed to the darkness, that he could dimly see some kind of a gate that they had gone through. Then the car picked up speed again, but not for long. There was a slight skid on gravel, as the driver jammed on the brakes, and the car came to a sudden stop. A brilliant light shone on the green of bushes, a few feet away from the radiator, as the headlights were switched on. They must have arrived at their destination.

'At least,' murmured Mr. Budd to himself. 'I've found the murderer — even if I'm not in a position to do much about it!'

The driver got down, came round to the door at the back, and jerked it open. The stout superintendent decided to pretend, for a moment, that he was still suffering from the effects of the drug. It might give him some advantage, though there wasn't much he could do, securely bound as he was. But you never could tell.

As the man opened the door, he rolled off the seat on to the floor with a grunt. The driver leaned inside the car and shook him gently. 'If only I'd got my hands free,' thought Mr. Budd, 'this'ud be me opportunity!' But all he could do was to remain limp.

The man shook him again, and getting no response caught him by the ankles and dragged him out over the running-board.

It was a most uncomfortable position, but the big man stuck it. The other paused for a moment, and then, stooping, he managed to get Mr. Budd across his back. This was no mean effort, for the stout superintendent was no lightweight.

Staggering a little, the driver carried him to some steps and through a door which he pushed open with his shoulder. Once inside, he dropped his heavy burden on a chair, shut the door, and switched on the light. Through half-shut eyes, Mr. Budd took stock of his surroundings.

He was in a spacious and well-appointed hall. A glance at the man who had brought him there disappointed him.

He was wearing goggles and a cloth cap that effectually concealed his identity. The big man had hoped to see his face. Well, perhaps there would be a chance later.

The man walked quickly to a door at the other end of the hall and pushed it open. For a moment he disappeared within. A dim light came on and he reappeared. Coming back to Mr. Budd, he half-dragged and half-carried him into the room. He hauled him on to a large couch and went out, shutting and locking the door behind him.

Mr. Budd allowed his eyes to open fully. A green shaded reading-lamp stood on a massive writing-table in the middle of the room and he knew that he had been brought to the same place that Janice Sheridan had been brought the first time.

'What's the next move, I wonder,' said Mr. Budd to himself. But his imagination didn't allow him to guess anything approaching the truth.

He examined the bonds that secured his arms and legs, and quickly discovered that they were stout leather straps, quite impossible to shift. They had been strapped so tightly that it was useless trying to loosen them one iota.

The key clicked in the lock, and the man came in again. Mr. Budd decided that he was tired of feigning unconsciousness.

'Nice place you've got here,' he remarked conversationally. 'But I don't like the way you treat your guests.'

'So you're awake, are you?' replied the other. He was still wearing the goggles and his cap, but he had discarded the heavy overcoat.

'That's pretty obvious,' grunted Mr. Budd.

'I'm glad, because I have something to say to you . . .'

'I know what it is,' interrupted the stout superintendent. 'But you're wastin' your time. I haven't got the key.'

'I never expected that you would have it on you,' retorted the other. 'But I am quite sure that you will get it for me.'

'Are you now?' remarked Mr. Budd sarcastically.

'Quite,' answered the man.

Mr. Budd shook his head slowly.

'If you was like me,' he said, 'you'd never be sure of anythin'. It's a bad habit, this bein' cocksure. But all murderers have got it. They're all cocksure — until the hangman straps their wrists on that last mornin' . . . '

'Be quiet, can't you?' snarled the other huskily. 'I don't want to listen to all that rubbish! The hangman won't get me.'

'I could give you a list as long as both your arms,' remarked Mr. Budd quietly, 'of people who've said the same thing. Shall I tell you where they are now . . . ?'

'No!' cried the man furiously. 'I don't want to hear! I don't care! I want that key, and I want it as soon as possible.'

'You'll have to break into Scotland Yard,' said Mr. Budd complacently. 'An' that isn't the easiest thing in the world . . . '

'Oh no, that's where you're wrong,' retorted the other. 'You will write a note to your sergeant and ask him to *bring* you the key.'

Mr. Budd laughed scornfully.

'D'you think I'm mad?' he inquired sarcastically.

'You will be mad if you don't,' said the man. 'I have a little gadget that I think will help you to change your mind.'

'Really?' Mr. Budd shook his head. 'For the sake of argument, supposin' I *did* write this note? D'you think that my sergeant would be such a fool as to come here alone? He's certain to know that something's wrong . . . '

'Don't let that worry you,' broke in the man. 'I've guarded against that. You will say that you are following an investigation and that you want the key at once. You will ask him to meet you at twelve o'clock tomorrow at Victoria Station under the clock.'

'An' when I'm not there? What then?' demanded the stout superintendent. 'He wouldn't hand the key to anyone else.'

'By the time he gets to the station,' answered the other smoothly, 'the key will no longer be in his possession.'

Mr. Budd stared at him blankly.

'You don't understand?' went on the man. 'It's really very simple. At Victoria

194

Station his pocket will be picked. I have arranged to pay for the services of an expert. Do you see how simple it is?'

Mr. Budd saw. It was certainly clever. If he wrote the letter there would be a good chance that it would come off.

'Not bad,' he agreed. 'But I've no intention of writin' that note.'

'We'll see.' The man went over to the door. 'I'll give you a couple of hours to think it over. When I come back I'll show you something that I'm sure will alter your ideas.'

He went out, locking the door on the outside.

Mr. Budd lay back on the couch and stared up at the ceiling. He was in a pretty bad mess. There was no use disguising that. What this man had in mind, he'd no idea, but it was something that he thought would ensure the success of his plan. Therefore, it was likely to prove distinctly unpleasant.

The stout superintendent had been in quite a few tight corners in his time, but this looked like equalling any of them.

His housekeeper would wonder what

had happened to him when he didn't come back. She knew that he had followed the youth who had brought the note, and she also knew that there was something wrong about it. She would notify the Yard. But how long would she wait before she did? She might think that he was still following up the youth. She wouldn't like to do anything that might upset his plans.

Of course, the whole thing had been done very cleverly. He had been *expected* to think there was something wrong about the note. The man had guessed that he wouldn't detain the youthful messenger but would do exactly what he had done, follow him. And walk into the prepared trap.

Very clever.

But what could he do *now*?

He tried again to loosen the straps at his wrists but they wouldn't budge. He was trussed up like a fowl for roasting, and he thought wryly, he might well be roasted if he couldn't think of a way of escape! The thought of writing the letter never even crossed his mind.

At the moment there was nothing to do but accept the situation and be ready for any chance that presented itself to turn the tables on the man who had brought him here.

It didn't seem like two hours before the man came back. He carried a large tin can which he set down carefully on the table. In his other hand he held a coil of thin rope.

Mr. Budd eyed both speculatively.

'Changed your mind?' inquired the man.

Mr. Budd shook his head.

'You'll be sorry,' said the other. He picked up the tin can, and the big man saw that it had a stout wire handle across the top, like a paint tin. The man took it over to the centre of the room, got up on a chair, and attached the wire holder carefully to the cord of the electic light fitting that hung from the ceiling. He got down and came over to the divan. He pulled at it until he had dragged it under the hanging tin, moving it about until he had got it in exactly the position he desired. Then he fetched the thin rope and bound the already helpless Mr. Budd to the divan so that it was impossible for him to move an inch.

'There,' he said, surveying his handi-work with satisfaction. 'Now we can get on with the rest of it. I'll explain what this all means. That can, over your head, has a small hole in the bottom. This hole is covered with a thin piece of zinc. I have here,' he produced from his pocket a glass-stoppered bottle, full of a colourless liquid, 'some pure sulphuric acid. I am going to pour it into that tin. When it has eaten its way through the zinc, which will not take very long, it will start to drip slowly. The hole is immediately above your eyes . . .'

Mr. Budd felt the perspiration break out on his forehead, but his fat face remained expressionless. He would not give the other the satisfaction of seeing the horror which swept over him.

The man climbed on the chair again, and very carefully poured the contents of the bottle into the tin can. He got down, moved the chair out of the way, and put the empty bottle on the table. Next, he took from his pocket a small bell of the kind that is operated by clockwork. This he placed in such a position under the stout superintendent's fingers that he could reach the press-stud.

'There,' he said. 'If between now and the falling of the first drop, you change your mind, press that bell and I will come at once. I should advise you to change your mind before it is too late.'

He crossed swiftly to the door and went out.

12

Given a specific job to do, the melancholy Sergeant Leek could be relied upon to carry it out conscientiously. He was anything but brilliant, but he was reliable and diligent when it came to following out a line of action. It was this that, in spite of his peculiarities, retained him his job. And there was no doubt that on many occasions luck favoured him.

It came heavily down on his side at Torbridge.

It was a very small village near Tavistock, and that was the nearest railway station. As soon as he arrived, he made himself known to the police at Tavistock, who were expecting him, but quickly discovered that they could offer no information that was likely to help him. Nobody had been reported missing at the date, eight years ago, that he was interested in.

Leek got a police car to take him to

Torbridge, and began his inquiries there. And, at first he met with a complete blank.

The accident was remembered but, when it came to anyone missing, there was nothing but shaking heads. The driver of the lorry responsible for the accident, was dead. The lean sergeant questioned a number of various people but he failed to get any further. There was one curious fact that emerged. Nobody seemed to remember the name of Sheridan at all. They remembered Renfrew but, apparently, had no recollection of Sheridan. Neither was there any record of the death of anyone named Sheridan in the registry of Births, Marriages, and Deaths, for the period. Here, he came upon a curious piece of information. There was a registration of a man named 'Wilmot' who had died in an accident on the same date. This had happened at Torbridge too. Leek could find no one who remembered there being *two* accidents on that date, and came to the conclusion that 'Wilmot' and 'Sheridan' were synonymous.

Was Sheridan calling himself Wilmot at the time or was Wilmot the actual man who had been run over? Leek made a further discovery. He succeeded in tracing the hotel in Tavistock where Renfrew had been staying at the time of the accident, and learned that Renfrew had been alone. Nobody had been with him.

But, according to the sergeant's information, Sheridan and Renfrew were supposed to have been together on holiday. That was what Janice Sheridan had told Mr. Budd.

But Renfrew had definitely been alone.

Leek had got so far when luck stepped in to help him. On the outskirts of Torbridge, he came upon a kind of caravan drawn up at the side of the road. An ancient and rather decrepit horse was grazing on a strip of grass, and the owner of the caravan, also ancient, and remarkably dirty, sat on the step smoking a pipe. The caravan was full of rush baskets, brooms made from tree-twigs, clothes-pegs, and other items, evidently for sale.

What induced the sergeant to stop and talk to the man with the pipe, he couldn't have said. But he did, and was very glad that he had.

After a preliminary conversation, Leek discovered that the man travelled round the country selling his goods to the outlying cottages and farms. Trade was not so good as it had been, but it was a living. He'd been doing it for most of his life. He travelled round most of the country. Yes, he'd been near Torbridge eight years ago, and he wasn't likely to forget it.

The interested Leek inquired what had happened.

The man took his pipe from his mouth and spat on the ground.

'Five quid 'e did me out of,' he answered. 'Me own brother-in-law too! If ever I get me 'ands on 'im I'll pay 'im out, or me name ain't Joe Garbit.'

'How did he do you out of five quid?' asked the sergeant.

Mr. Garbit spat again.

'Give it 'im to get some bacca an' things,' he said. 'I'd 'urt me ankle on these 'ere dratted steps. A five pund note it were. Never come back, 'e didn't. Ain't seen 'im from that day to this. Cleared off with me five pund an' never come back.'

Mr. Garbit spat for the third time to signify his disgust.

'Do you remember the exact date?' asked Leek.

'Do I remember me own name?' demanded Joe Garbit. 'Wouldn't you remember the 'zact date that you was done outer a five pund note by a thievin' rascal? 'Course I does . . . '

He was so incensed at the idea that he could forget when such an outrage had happened, that he omitted to mention the date, but, when he finally did, Leek was jubilant.

It was the day of the accident!

It must have been Mr. Garbit's brother-in-law who had been run over by the lorry! He wouldn't have been missed because Mr. Garbit believed that he had run off with the money.

Leek obtained all the particulars he could. The name of the 'absconding' brother-in-law was Bob Linker. Mr. Garbit couldn't even pronounce it without showing his displeasure by several vicious spits. Then he grew suddenly suspicious.

"'Ere,' he demanded, 'why are yer askin' all these 'ere questions for? You don't know nuthin' about Bob Linker, does yer?'

'I think you may be wrong about his pinchin' your fiver,' said Leek and explained.

When he had got a signed statement from the surprised Mr. Garbit, he caught the next train back to London, congratulating himself on his cleverness in having successfully carried out his mission.

★ ★ ★

Mr. Budd had underestimated his housekeeper when he thought that that dour woman would delay taking any action in case she should be interfering with any plans of his own. She was accustomed to doing what she considered the right thing, irrespective of what effect it might have on anyone else.

And so she rang up Scotland Yard and reported exactly what had happened.

This was relayed to Detective-Inspector MacGregor who immediately rang her back for further details. These she supplied, with such an accurate description of the youth who had brought the note, that MacGregor felt he could have recognised him instantly.

There was, as yet, no alarm felt for the stout superintendent. MacGregor concluded that he was following up the line that had fallen so luckily into his hands. But at the same time, he decided that there could be no harm in having the youth pulled in, if he could be found.

He was found, later that night, in a coffee bar in Soho where he had roused the suspicions of the proprietor by trying to change a five pound note. There was no doubt that he was the same youth. The vigilant eyes of the housekeeper had noticed a crescent-shaped scar on his forehead between his thick brows, which she had duly included in her detailed description.

The youth was brought to MacGregor and questioned, and it was from what he had to tell that the first real alarm for the safety of Mr. Budd, started.

At first, the unpleasant youth, whose name was Swales, tried to bluster. He denied that he had ever taken a note to Mr. Budd's house in Streatham. Threatened, however, with being detained in Cannon Row police station for further investigation, he told all he knew.

He had been approached by a man he swore he had never seen before, and asked to take the note to Mr. Budd. The man had given him two five-pound notes and had driven him to the end of the road in a car. He had told him that there might be some trouble, but that he wouldn't have to worry because, he, the man in the car, would be close at hand. He instructed him what to do and say, and promised him a further ten pounds if he did his job well.

He had done what he'd been told, and that was all he knew about it. The stranger had expected that the big man would let him go and follow him, and this is what had happened.

Swales denied at first that he knew anything more, but when he was pressed, admitted that he had waited to get his other ten pounds, and had actually seen the cloth thrown over Mr. Budd's head and the big man dragged into the waiting car. The man had paid him the other ten pounds. He had no idea who he was, or anything else about him. He had met him in a coffee bar, and that was the first time he had ever seen him. The description he gave tallied with Janice Sheridan's description of the man who had kidnapped her.

Swales had a record for petty theft and violence, and MacGregor detained him for further questioning.

Hoppy arrived at Scotland Yard later that night. He had telephoned Mr. Budd's house, to see if there was any further news of the case, from his office in Fleet Street, and heard what had happened from the housekeeper. He succeeded, after some difficulty, in seeing MacGregor.

'I've noo time for reporters,' grunted the inspector. 'I've a lot of wairk to . . . '

'All right,' interrupted Hoppy, puffing furiously at one of his eternal Woodbines.

'I know. But I'm worried . . . '

'I'm worried mesel',' growled MacGregor.

'What are you doing?' asked Hoppy. 'This may be serious. This man has got Budd, and there's no doubt why. He wants that key . . . '

'Weel, he'll noo get it,' said MacGregor curtly.

'But what's going to happen to Budd?' demanded the reporter. 'We've got to do something quickly. We've got to find him.'

'Aye,' agreed the inspector, 'but will ye tell me how? We've noo ideear who this man is, or where he's to be found. If the superintendent's ideear aboot the key . . . '

'What was that?' broke in Hoppy sharply.

'I'm no prepared to discuss it with a reporter,' retorted MacGregor sternly.

Hoppy made a gesture of impatience.

'Never mind all that,' he cried. 'Tell me! You know I've been working with Budd over this case. Don't be obstinate, man! It may be important. I want to help.'

'Weel,' said MacGregor relenting a little. 'The superintendent considered that the key might belong to a safe deposit . . . '

'Of course!' In his excitement Hoppy almost shouted. 'What a fool I've been not to have thought of that . . . '

'Inquiries have been made at nearly every safe deposit in London,' put in the inspector, 'and there's noo one of 'em with a client of the name of Haines, Gilmore, or Sheridan . . . '

'We've got to find that safe deposit,' said Hoppy. 'That's where the tapes are. Budd must've guessed that. And this man is after them because they contain the whole story . . . '

'Ye mean the story that involves the mairderer?' said MacGregor.

Hoppy nodded quickly.

'Of course,' he said, stubbing out his Woodbine and lighting another. 'The story that was also in the play. We've got to find the safe deposit . . . '

'If it exists,' remarked the inspector gloomily.

'I'm sure it does,' said the reporter.

'Budd thought so, and he's always right.'

He stopped suddenly. An idea had leapt to his mind.

'Can I use the phone?' he asked.

'What's in your mind?' inquired MacGregor.

'I want to get on to Janice Sheridan,' answered Hoppy. 'I believe we've all overlooked something obvious.'

MacGregor assented grudgingly. It was only because he was genuinely worried about Mr. Budd that he brooked any interference on the part of a newspaper man. A few seconds later, Hoppy was speaking to Janice.

'I want you to tell me the name of your father, Miss Sheridan,' he said quickly. 'Is it Sheridan, or did you take Sheridan for a stage name?'

'My father's name was Wilmot,' she answered. 'That is my real name . . . '

'Your father's Christian name?'

'Charles. What . . . ?'

'I've no time to explain now,' said Hoppy. 'Thanks.' He put down the telephone and turned to MacGregor. 'That's why you couldn't find the safe deposit. You'd got the wrong name. Charles Wilmot is the name you want.'

★　★　★

Mr. Budd lay quite still and fixed his eyes on the deadly tin that hung above his head. It possessed a horrible kind of fascination for him.

How long would it be before the acid ate through the zinc? Over and over again, he imagined that he could see a drop forming at the bottom of the tin. Soon it would no longer be imagination, but reality.

Mr. Budd was anything but a superman. He was an ordinary human being, neither better nor worse than most. But he was stubborn. He would not be forced by fear to comply with the demand of this man.

But he was really frightened.

He knew something of the effects of pure sulphuric acid. It destroyed flesh and tissue. He had once seen the results of a vitriol-throwing and the face of the victim had remained long in his memory . . .

He tried to distract his mind by thinking of ways of escape. But he couldn't think of any. There might be a chance that he would be found in time, but it was a very slender one. Unless the inquiries he had set in motion regarding the safe deposit, and the key, bore fruit.

He was quite convinced that the recorded tapes had been put there, and that they contained the whole story of the murder of Wurtz, and also the name of the murderer.

Renfrew?

Yes, he thought there was little doubt that the man who had murdered Sheridan, Loveridge, and Maitland, was Renfrew, desperately trying to cover up for that other murder — the murder of Wurtz. He hadn't got the whole of the story yet, but that was the basic outline. There were a lot of bits to fill up, a lot of loose ends to tie neatly, but he was pretty sure that he was right, in the main.

This man, who had brought him here, was Renfrew.

He had nearly tackled him with it, but thought it was better not to give away the fact that he knew so much.

His eyes sought the tin again. The bottom was dry and smooth. The acid had not done its job of eating through the zinc yet. He couldn't repress a shudder as he thought what it would be like when the first drop fell. It might miss his eyes, but the agony would be terrible, even on the flesh of his face.

Mr. Budd prayed that if the worst came to the worst, he would never recover from the ordeal. It would be better to die than to live the rest of his life a faceless, sightless thing . . .

The perspiration was running down his cheeks and his body felt hot and clammy. He tried to move but he couldn't. The cords held him like a vice and the straps prevented him from being able to shift them.

How much longer would it be?

He had no idea how long the acid would take. It depended on the thickness of the zinc.

It was no good thinking about it, and, with an effort, he forced his mind away again. How had Leek got on at Torbridge?

Had he succeeded in finding the man who had been buried for Sheridan?

Poor old Leek! He was always taking a rise out of him, but they had worked together for a long time and they more or less understood one another. He was a good man at his job when he liked to put his mind to it. All these notions he got into his head were really a kind of wishful thinking — a kind of elaborate daydreaming. He wanted to be more than he had the abilities to attain . . .

He wondered what time it was. He couldn't see the watch on his wrist or the clock in the room. He tried to calculate how long he had been there, but gave it up. It seemed a very long time but it couldn't be . . .

How far was the acid from eating through the zinc?

That was an ever present thought at the back of his brain. How long?

There was nothing he could do about it, anyhow. He might as well make up his mind to face the ordeal with as much courage as he could muster. He almost wished that it would break through quickly and get it done with. This waiting was terrible.

His arms and legs were numb from the confining straps, and he was beginning to suffer the agony of cramp.

And then he saw a suspicion of moisture in the middle of the bottom of the suspended tin. He wasn't sure, but he thought he saw it — a slightly darker spot. Almost holding his breath he strained his eyes to make certain. But he could not be sure. The light from the reading-lamp was not very bright. He closed his eyes and looked again . . .

There was no doubt! A tiny pin-point of liquid had appeared. The acid had penetrated the zinc! It couldn't be long before the drop grew too heavy to hang suspended, and fell!

It would take a little while. Sulphuric acid is a viscous liquid. But it couldn't be very long.

With a fixed stare that hurt his eyes, Mr. Budd watched the tiny drop of fluid. Slowly, very slowly, it got bigger and bigger and he had to bite his lips to prevent himself from screaming. His fingers touched the bell. He had only to press the button and there would be a respite from this soul-destroying tension. The sound of the bell would bring Renfrew at once. He stopped himself with an almost superhuman effort. It would do no good in the long run. Renfrew would never be such a fool as to let him leave this place alive . . .

But surely anything was better than the corroding acid?

It was quite impossible to avoid the acid falling on him. He had tried how far he could shift his head and found that he could only move it sideways.

The drops would fall slowly at first and then, as the acid ate away more and more of the zinc, would come faster and faster until they became a continuous stream.

The cramp had knotted the muscles in his legs and the pain was so intense that he tried to ease it by moving his foot, the only portion of his body that he could move. He thrust his foot forward, pointing his toes like a ballet dancer. And his foot touched the leg of the big writing-table!

Mr. Budd raised his head as far as it would go. He could just see his feet. The right shoe had brushed the side of the table leg! If he twisted it sideways, the sole of his shoe would come in contact with the leg of the table.

Mr. Budd breathed a silent prayer. The divan on which he lay was on casters. If he could thrust his foot against the table leg with sufficient force, he might be able to push the divan further back. It wouldn't be very far, but enough to avoid the acid from falling on his face. But there would only be *one* chance. If he didn't succeed the first time, there would be no opportunity to try again.

Very cautiously, gritting his teeth against the pain of his cramp, he turned his right foot sideways until the sole was flat against the table leg.

And then, with every atom of strength he could muster, he pushed!

The divan moved. It slid back and, at the same moment, the first drop of acid from the tin fell!

But it missed Mr. Budd's face and fell on the rope that bound him to the divan.

A surge of relief swept over the stout superintendent as he realised what had happened. For the time being, at least, he had been saved.

And then he realised something else.

The acid was eating through the rope!

It was turning yellow and becoming pulpy! He waited for a moment and then he arched his body upward against the restraining rope. The strand where the acid had fallen, parted! He felt the rest loosen slightly. With all his strength, he pressed upward again and again until, at last, the rope was so loose that he could wriggle free.

But he was still helpless from the straps at his wrists and ankles. The worst danger from the acid, however, was postponed. His eyes and his face were safe.

He lay back, limp from his exertions and the reaction.

He had gained a breathing space. Sooner or later, of course, Renfrew would come back to see what had happened, but until then he was out of immediate danger.

A second drop of acid fell and another

was gathering. Mr. Budd rolled himself off the divan on to the floor. The dripping acid would now fall on the divan, burning into it, but leaving him unharmed.

If only he could get free from those infernal straps! But that was beyond him. He had tried so many times before, and he knew that nothing he could do would budge them.

And then he heard a sound that he had both expected and dreaded. It was the sound of a footstep outside the door, followed by the click of the key in the lock.

Renfrew was coming back!

14

A small army of detective officers scoured all the known safe deposits in London, and their task was not made any easier by the fact that the managers had gone home, and had to be routed out and questioned.

Luckily, safe deposits are not so plentiful. There are comparatively few. There was always the chance, of course, that the key belonged to a private safe in a bank, but this was something it would have been impossible to cope with.

Hoppy, consuming Woodbine after Woodbine, in an agony of nervous impatience, waited in Detective-Inspector MacGregor's office for the reports to come in.

Time was the essence of the inquiry. Mr. Budd might be in considerable danger, and every second counted.

Of course, there was always the possibility that the stout superintendent had been wrong about the key. It might not belong to a safe deposit at all, and, even if it did, and they found the safe, it might not contain what they expected.

Three negative reports came in, and then they got a lucky break.

Detective-Sergeant Oxley telephoned to say that he had found a safe in the Fetter Lane deposit that had been rented for the past ten years in the name of Charles Wilmot.

'It may not be our man, sir,' said the sergeant, 'but I think it's likely. I've got the manager here. Will you come along and bring the key?'

A police car raced Hoppy and MacGregor to Fetter Lane. They found Oxley with the rather disgruntled manager, who had been brought from his home just as he was on the point of going to bed.

'This is all very irregular,' he grumbled, 'but in view of what this officer tells me, I suppose I had better waive the rules.'

'Here is the key,' said MacGregor. 'Is it one of yours?'

The manager peered at it, and nodded.
'Yes, it's one of our keys,' he said. 'I'll

take you to the safe.'

They followed him down in the lift to the vault. This was entered by a heavy steel door, with an intricate combination lock, which the manager opened. Beyond was a reinforced concrete passage, the walls of which were lined with small steel doors on each of which was painted a number.

'This is the safe you want,' said the manager, going to number sixteen. 'This was rented by Charles Wilmot.'

He inserted the key in the lock and it turned easily. They pressed forward as he gently pulled the safe door open.

Was this going to be a fiasco, or would the contents turn out to be what they were after?

At first sight the safe appeared empty, and then they saw the two reels of tape on the single shelf, and a sealed envelope.

'The missing tapes,' cried Hoppy excitedly. 'Budd was right!'

They gave the manager a receipt for the tapes and the letter, and raced back to Scotland Yard. The letter was addressed to Janice Sheridan. In red ink were the instructions: *'To be opened after my death'*.

'How did he expect her to get it?' asked MacGregor. 'The mon must've been crazy . . . '

'Never mind that,' broke in the reporter. 'Play back those tapes. That's what we want.'

The tape-recorder was started and the voice of a dead man, clear and lifelike, came from the loudspeaker.

And as they listened, the mystery was a mystery no longer. The identity of the man who had killed the man whose voice they were listening to, Phyllida Loveridge, and Guy Maitland, was revealed. And he was to be found within an hour's journey of Scotland Yard.

★ ★ ★

The man, still wearing the goggles and cap, came into the room. He uttered a sharp exclamation when he saw the empty divan, and then his eyes moved down to Mr. Budd on the floor. He came over quickly.

'How did you get off the divan?' he demanded. 'I tied you very firmly . . . '

'You're not up to all the dodges,' said Mr. Budd. 'I expect you're a bit disappointed. Thought you'd find me writhin' in agony . . . '

'That is only delayed,' retorted the man. 'Unless, of course, you're willing to write that letter . . . ?'

'I'm not,' broke in the stout superintendent curtly.

'Then we'll continue with the method of persuasion,' said Renfrew. He stopped and dragged Mr. Budd back on to the divan.

'I see that you managed to shift it,' he said. 'I don't know how you did it, but it makes no difference. I can soon push it back in its former place . . . '

And at that moment there sounded through the stillness of the house a thunderous knocking! Mr. Budd's pulses jumped. Was it possible that the police had found him?

Renfrew straightened up. His hand went quickly to his pocket. He turned and stared at the door.

'Hadn't you better see who it is?' inquired the stout superintendent, as the knocking was repeated. 'I've got an idea that some friends o' mine have dropped in to see me.'

Renfrew's hand came out of his pocket holding a small automatic pistol. He turned it toward Mr. Budd.

'If I'm going to swing, I'll swing for you as well,' he said thickly, and his finger tightened on the trigger. There came a rending crash from the window and the tinkle of breaking glass.

Renfrew pulled the trigger, but the shock destroyed his aim. The bullet whined over Mr. Budd's head. Renfrew was breathing heavily as though he had been running. The curtains at the smashed window were torn down, and Hoppy leapt into the room. He was followed by two constables.

Renfrew fired and one of the policemen gave a cry of pain, clapped his hand to his leg, and crumpled up on the floor. Before the man could fire again the other man was on him, gripping him by the pistol wrist and trying to force the weapon from his grip. They began to struggle backwards and forwards, each striving to get hold of the weapon.

Hoppy made for Mr. Budd. With his pocket-knife he slashed at the straps and succeeded in cutting the big man's hands free.

'All right,' grunted Mr. Budd. 'I can get these things off my ankles. See if you can help that feller.'

Hoppy turned to see what was happening. The constable and the man in goggles were still fighting desperately. The policeman was doing his utmost to prevent the other from turning the automatic against him. Locked together, they swayed into the centre of the room.

They staggered into the divan just as Mr. Budd unstrapped his ankles and got gingerly to his feet. They fell together, the policeman underneath, across the divan. The shock of the fall jarred Renfrew's elbow, and the automatic went off. The shot hit the ceiling, bringing down a little shower of plaster. By an effort, the constable succeeded in wrenching himself free. Renfrew fired again as the policeman flung himself backwards. The bullet struck the wire supporting the deadly tin of sulphuric acid. It fell, straight on to the face of Renfrew who was lying directly beneath.

He received the contents of the tin in one burning deluge full on his face! His shriek of agony was dreadful. He writhed onto the floor, tearing at the goggles which had failed to protect his eyes from the acid, and scream after scream filled the room.

'Quick, we must do somethin',' cried Mr. Budd. 'He'll be burnt to pulp.'

'What is it, sir?' asked the constable, looking in horror at the thing that was twisting and turning and moaning on the floor.

'Sulphuric acid,' said Mr. Budd. 'Go and see if you can find some water.'

The constable ran out of the room without a word, just as Detective-Inspector MacGregor came through the shattered window.

'Have ye got the man?' he demanded, and Mr. Budd pointed to the figure on the floor.

'What's the mattair with him?' asked MacGregor.

The cries of the poor wretch had sunk to low, shuddering sobs, as the stout superintendent briefly explained.

'Poor devil!' grunted MacGregor. 'Though I mind it sairves him right. What's the mattair with you Fuller?'

He moved over to the wounded constable who was tenderly nursing his leg.

'Only a flesh wound, sir,' he answered with a wry smile. 'Bullet went through me calf.'

'We'll get ye to a doctor as soon as possible,' promised the inspector. 'What can we do with this other mon?'

The second policeman came back carrying a bowl of water and a towel. Mr. Budd took it from him and went over to Renfrew. He was only making faint moaning sounds now, and moving convulsively.

The big man knelt down stiffly. His legs still hurt him from the confinement of the straps. Renfrew had pulled away the goggles and the sight that met Mr. Budd's gaze was terrible. It was a long time afterwards before he forgot it.

The face was a glutinous pulp. Of the eyes little remained but a blur . . . Even as Mr. Budd looked down, he gave a last shuddering sigh and was still.

The stout superintendent laid his hand on the other's chest. He shook his head.

'Is he dead?' asked Hoppy.

'Yes,' answered Mr. Budd. 'The shock, I suppose.'

'Weel,' remarked MacGregor, 'it will have saved the hangman a job.'

Mr. Budd, very gently, pulled up the left trouser leg and looked at the knee.

'That's enough evidence to prove that the man was Walter Renfrew,' he remarked.

'How did you know?' demanded Hoppy. 'We only knew it was Renfrew just over an hour ago.'

'Renfrew suffered from a fractured knee-cap that wasn't properly set,' answered Mr. Budd. 'I knew the murderer limped slightly on his left leg from those foot-prints at Barnet. When Miss Sheridan told me that Renfrew had a fractured knee-cap, it was pretty obvious.'

He got heavily to his feet and spread his handkerchief over the travesty of a face.

'It's lucky we've somethin' to identify him from,' he said. 'The acid hasn't left much else.'

14

A week had elapsed since Walter Renfrew had died in such a terrible manner, and during that period, Mr. Budd had been a very busy man indeed sorting and arranging the scattered fragments of the puzzle.

A Home Office order resulted in the exhumation of the body of the man who had been buried under the name of Charles Wilmot eight years previously, and the measurements of the body, or more correctly the skeleton, proved beyond doubt that it was not Wilmot. It was a much shorter man altogether. There was, unfortunately, nothing to show whether it was the missing Bob Linker, but, taking the date and other circumstances into consideration, it was only reasonable to conclude that it was.

The main thing, however, was to prove that it was not Wilmot, and this had been conclusive.

Although Mr. Budd knew beyond doubt that it couldn't have been, the exhumation had been necessary from the legal aspect.

This, and other facts connected with the case, including the statement recorded by Wilmot on the tapes found in the safe deposit, enabled the stout superintendent to piece the whole extraordinary story together and resolve it into a coherent whole.

And a very curious and unusual story it was. Mr. Budd made a verbal report to the assistant commissioner, in the latter's office, and Colonel Blair, dapper and immaculate as ever, listened with great interest.

'Most of what I'm goin' to tell you, sir,' said Mr. Budd, wedged uncomfortably in a chair in front of the desk, 'is recorded on the tapes made by Charles Wilmot an' deposited by him in the Fetter Lane safe deposit. That gave us all the details. The things he didn't include, I've managed to fill in. It was a queer business altogether.'

'But, as usual, you got to the bottom of it,' remarked Colonel Blair.

'It seemed a bit of a jumble at one

time,' said Mr. Budd. 'All these different names that Wilmot adopted was rather confusin', but I've got it all plain now. I must admit, though, that it's one of the strangest cases I've ever had to deal with.'

'The kind of case that's just up your street,' interposed the assistant commissioner. 'I said so at the beginning, if you remember.'

Mr. Budd nodded.

'I hope the next is goin' to be somethin' a bit more simple,' he replied. 'It 'ud make a change.' He cleared his throat. 'Well, sir, to get down to the facts. This feller, Walter Renfrew, was a school friend of Wilmot's. They was practically brought up together. It seems that they was almost inseparable up to the time of Wilmot's twenty-fifth birthday, when Renfrew got a job abroad an' was away for several years.

'Wilmot was pretty well off, he'd had quite a bit o' money left him by his father, but Renfrew was always more or less broke. He'd had a number o' jobs but he never stuck to any of 'em, an' was always in trouble of some kind.'

'A thoroughly bad hat,' murmured Colonel Blair.

'That's right,' assented the big man. 'Most of his troubles was money. He had extravagant tastes without the means of gratifyin' 'em. Wilmot, apparently, helped him out of some very unpleasant positions, over an' over again. You'd've thought that this feller, Renfrew, would've been grateful, but he wasn't. Well, durin' the time that Renfrew was away abroad, Wilmot got married to Miss Janice Sheridan's mother. P'raps, I should say to the woman who was to be her mother. This seems to have been the start of the whole business. Renfrew got the sack from his job abroad an' came back to England, broke as usual, an' heavily in debt, also as usual. And he fell violently in love with Wilmot's wife.'

Mr. Budd paused. He dipped into the pocket of his waistcoat and fingered one of his black cigars, longingly. Colonel Blair saw the action and smiled. But he didn't suggest that the stout superintendent should smoke. There were, he thought, limits to a man's endurance, and

Mr. Budd's cigars were beyond it.

'Renfrew fell in love with Mrs. Wilmot,' continued the big man, 'an' he made up his mind that he'd get her for himself. There was a bit more to it than just love, I think, because he found out that an aunt of hers, a very rich woman, was leavin' all her money to her niece when she died, an' this was more at the root of his determination to marry her than love. What happened later seems to bear this out. But Renfrew was the type that the unattainable attracted, an' added spice to his attempt to get it.'

'There are a lot of men like that,' commented the assistant commissioner. 'Go on.'

'It seems,' said Mr. Budd, dutifully 'going on', 'that any friendly feelin's he ever had for Wilmot turned to hatred now that the man was in his way. He must've spent most of his time schemin' to try an' hit on a plan that would get him out of the way. He'd probably have murdered him then, only it wouldn't've done what he wanted. An' then a bit o' luck came to his help.

'Wilmot had been speculating in shares and his speculations proved disastrous. Most of his income was swallowed up, an' he had to find a large sum to meet his liabilities to his brokers. He was unwilling to touch his capital, an' he'd already got an overdraft at his bank. He decided to borrow the money he wanted from a moneylender.'

'Wurtz?' put in Colonel Blair.

Mr. Budd nodded.

'He told Renfrew what he was contemplatin', an' asked him if he knew a moneylender he could go to. From past experience, Wilmot was sure that Renfrew *would* know one. Renfrew appeared only too pleased to help, but he saw, at last, the opportunity he had been waitin' for. He could kill two birds with one stone — rid himself of Wilmot in a most satisfactory way, an' also get himself out of trouble.

'He sent Wilmot to Joseph Wurtz. Wurtz agreed, on the security Wilmot offered, to grant him a loan of five thousand pounds for a period of three months. Wilmot was delighted. He was able to settle his accounts with his brokers an' retain the shares which he was sure would pick up. He didn't know that Renfrew had also borrowed a large sum of money from Wurtz, neither did he know that he had done so on forged securities, a fact that Wurtz had discovered and was threatening Renfrew with either the return of his money or arrest for fraud.

'It was impossible for Renfrew to find the money, an' so it was necessary to silence Wurtz. There was only one way to do that . . . '

'Murder, eh?' said the assistant commissioner, nodding his sleek grey head. 'I'm beginning to see.'

'He'd already decided to kill Wurtz when Wilmot asked him if he knew a moneylender, an' his plan, in a nutshell, was to murder Wurtz and lay the blame on Wilmot. He saw Wurtz and begged him for three months' grace, promising that he would repay all he owed him plus interest. Wurtz agreed. All he was interested in was gettin' his money back, an' three months wouldn't make much difference. He could always take action if

Renfrew didn't keep his word.

'Renfrew's outward friendliness with Wilmot had never changed, so that he was able to learn all Wilmot's plans. The shares had suddenly boomed, and Wilmot found that he had made sufficient money to repay his loan to Wurtz, and a considerable profit as well. Anxious to get the loan cleared, Wilmot made an appointment with Wurtz to settle up the business. Wurtz suggested his private house. He had learned that Renfrew was a friend of Wilmot's and he wanted to warn him. He was goin' to do this after their business had been finished, an' thought his house was a better place than his office. Wilmot agreed, although he had no idea of the moneylender's reason.

'Naturally, he told Renfrew about the appointment, an' it was just what Renfrew had been waitin' for . . . '

Colonel Blair pursed up his lips.

'Supposing there had been no appointment?' he asked. 'What then?'

'Well, sir,' said Mr. Budd, 'I think he'd have found some other way. But the appointment *was* made, an' the plan was thrown in his lap, as you might say. Wilmot didn't want his bank to know anything about his dealin' with Wurtz, Wurtz's name was pretty well known, an' so he took the five thousand in cash, instead of givin' a cheque. He was goin' to pay the interest on the loan, later, when he'd found out the exact amount that Wurtz was chargin'.

'Renfrew followed Wilmot when he kept the appointment. He made his way round to the back of the house an' tied a scarf round his face. In the middle of the interview, he suddenly threw open the window, shot Wurtz, an' flung the revolver into the room. Wilmot, shocked and surprised, picked up the weapon an' fired at the unknown man — unknown to him, I mean. The bullet hit the window frame. An' at that moment, Neate burst in . . . '

'The result was a foregone conclusion,' said the assistant commissioner. 'Wilmot, with the revolver in his hand, and the dead body of Wurtz slumped across the desk. No wonder Wilmot was accused of the murder.'

'Exactly, sir,' agreed Mr. Budd. 'Everythin' accordin' to plan. But then things went wrong. Wilmot, to avoid a scandal that would have involved his wife, gave a false name, John Gilmore. He hoped that the whole thing would soon be put straight, an' in the meantime he'd keep it from his wife who was ill. Renfrew hadn't bargained for this. He had hoped that Wilmot's name would be mud, so that he, Renfrew, would have a better chance with Mrs. Wilmot. There wasn't much he could do about it, unless he gave Wilmot's real name to the police, an' he didn't want to get mixed up in it. His own relations with the dead money-lender might've come out an' led to inquiries. But he went to see Wilmot while he was waitin' his trial, an' Wilmot asked him if he would post a letter to his wife from Torbridge. To account for his absence he'd told her that he was on a short holiday with Renfrew.

'Renfrew tried to dissuade him from keepin' up the 'John Gilmore' alias, but Wilmot was adamant. On no account must this ghastly mistake reach the ears of his wife. And Renfrew, in whose brain a fresh scheme was maturin', an' who was practically certain that Wilmot would hang, agreed to keep the secret.

'He went down to Torbridge and posted the letter which Wilmot had given him, an', just as he posted it, a man was run over at the corner by a heavy lorry. The lorry had crushed the man's head, an' always an opportunist, Renfrew claimed the dead man as his friend, Charles Wilmot.'

'It was a risk, surely?' said Colonel Blair. 'The dead man might have been known . . .'

'He mighter been, but he wasn't,' said Mr. Budd. 'Renfrew's luck held. Renfrew made all the arrangements for the burial, an' while Wilmot, in the name of Gilmore, was awaitin' his trial, Mrs. Wilmot was lyin' seriously ill from the shock of his supposed death.'

'A very pretty little plan,' remarked Colonel Blair. 'What a thorough-paced scoundrel the man was.'

'Not a nice feller at all,' said the stout superintendent. 'But he didn't get it quite all his own way. Instead of a verdict of wilful murder, Wilmot got off with manslaughter an' robbery an' a fifteen year sentence. It must've given Renfrew a nasty shock. I'll bet he spent some uncomfortable moments wonderin' if Wilmot, at the last, would give away his real identity. But Wilmot stuck to his guns. As John Gilmore he'd been arrested, an' as John Gilmore he went through with it. Renfrew could breathe again. As far as his wife an' daughter was concerned, Wilmot was dead — an' buried.'

'And Renfrew 'married' the widow,' murmured the assistant commissioner.

'That's right, sir,' said Mr. Budd. 'An', true to type, havin' got what he wanted, he no longer wanted it. But he wanted the money that Mrs. Renfrew inherited from her aunt, an' he got it. Then he deserted her an' completely disappeared.'

'That, I presume, is what you'd call the end of part one, eh?' said Colonel Blair, as the big man paused.

'That's the end of part one, sir,' agreed Mr. Budd. 'An' part two begins when

Wilmot escaped from prison. Durin' his sentence his great anxiety had been his wife an' daughter, but he believed implicitly in Renfrew's promise that he would look after them. He could offer no reason for his apparent desertion, but he had arranged with Renfrew, who visited him twice in prison, using the name of Roger Clayton, to assure his family that he was well and it was only force of circumstances that kept him away. He had plenty of money. Not even Renfrew knew of the safe deposit in Fetter Lane, and there was money there — nearly ten thousand pounds. Enough to see him out of the country. But he had to see his wife first. He had made up his mind to tell her the truth . . . '

'It's a pity he didn't do it in the beginning,' grunted Colonel Blair. 'It would have saved a great many lives, including his own.'

'I suppose his attitude was understandable, sir. He didn't think it would become serious. He never imagined that his story wouldn't be believed. When it wasn't, it was too late to go back.'

'Well, it was foolish, all the same,' said the assistant commissioner. 'How does this play come into it? That's what I want to know.'

'I'm comin' to that,' said Mr. Budd. 'On his escape, Wilmot, paid a visit to the safe deposit an' got his money. Still believing in the integrity of Renfrew, he made his way to the house where he had been livin' at the time of the moneylender's murder. But he found other people there.

'After a few careful inquiries he learned of his supposed death, of his wife's remarriage and subsequent death, an' bit by bit he unearthed Renfrew's treachery.'

'I can imagine what he felt like, poor devil,' remarked the assistant commissioner sympathetically.

'I should say if he could've got his hands on Renfrew, he'd've killed him,' said Mr. Budd. 'He suspected, for the first time, that Renfrew had killed Wurtz and 'framed' him for the crime. He was nearly mad with rage against the man who had betrayed him. In the meantime, Renfrew had returned to England from abroad. He had somehow, an' I'll bet it was some crooked business, got hold of quite a large sum of money. He bought a house in Barnet in the name of Roger Clayton, an' was living in comfort. He felt quite secure, for Wilmot had still a good many years of his sentence to run. An' then he read in the newspapers an account of the escape of John Gilmore, an' his feelin' of security fled.

'But he could do nothin' because he hadn't the faintest idea where the man was. Wilmot, however, was better informed. He had discovered the whereabouts of his betrayer. Renfrew had been foolish to stick to the name Roger Clayton, the same he had used when he visited Wilmot in prison, an' this gave him away.

'Wilmot, in the name of Jonathan Haines, took a house also in Barnet. In fact, not very far away from Renfrew's. Here, he planned out his revenge. At first, he says in the statement he recorded on the tapes, he intended to kill Renfrew. But he thought of a better plan. He wrote the whole story of the murder of Wurtz, and Renfrew's perfidy, in the form of a play. It was all set down in detail, an' he used the actual names of the people concerned . . . '

'He'd have never got it produced,' interpolated Colonel Blair. 'It wouldn't have got past the Lord Chamberlain.'

'I don't suppose he thought of that,' said Mr. Budd. 'Anyway, it would have roused the curiosity of anyone who read it. Wilmot couldn't go out during the day in case he was recognised by Renfrew, or, worse still, by the police who were looking for him. But he used to go out at night, an' invariably went over to Renfrew's house to gloat over the coming downfall of the man who had caused him so much misery.'

'You really are telling this extremely well,' said the assistant commissioner. 'I congratulate you.'

Mr. Budd reddened slightly.

'I'm quotin' most of it, sir,' he answered a little stiffly, 'from the man's own statement. Well, on one of these night prowlin's, he was seen an' recognised by Renfrew. Renfrew's previous fear became a panic. While Wilmot was alive he was in danger. He decided that the only thing to do was to kill him, his way out of any difficulty. He found out by discreet inquiries that Wilmot was livin' at King's Lodge.

'Mind you, he knew nothin' as yet concernin' the play which Wilmot had completed and sent to Phyllida Loveridge for typin' with instructions to send one copy to Maitland. Neither did he know that Wilmot had dictated the full details of his story to a tape-recorder, an' put the tapes in his safe deposit in Fetter Lane. He sent the key to his daughter, who he discovered was now a leadin' actress at a West End theatre, and wrote down the use it was to be put to in a sealed envelope, addressed to his daughter, which he locked in a drawer of his desk. He put a duplicate letter with the tapes in the safe at the safe deposit . . . '

'Careful chap, Wilmot,' said Colonel Blair. 'He believed in taking precautions . . . '

'They didn't save him, poor feller,' replied Mr. Budd. 'Renfrew succeeded in killin' him.'

'How did he know about the play and the tapes?' asked the assistant commissioner.

'He found the letter that Wilmot had left for his daughter,' said Mr. Budd. 'He searched the place an' there were probably a lot o' notes about the play, which he destroyed. He must've found a note to the effect that it had been sent to Phyllida Loveridge for typin'. He'd got to find an' destroy that play an' silence anyone who might've read it.

'Well, we know what he did. He found the bill which told him that a copy had been sent to Maitland. He dealt with him and got hold of the only copy left of the play. As one lie leads to another, Renfrew had to commit murder after murder to cover up. An' he still had to get the key of the safe deposit an' destroy those tapes.' Mr. Budd drew a long breath. 'I think that's about the lot, sir,' he said with satisfaction. 'I've got my written report ready for you, but I thought you'd like to hear the story from me first.'

Colonel Blair lay back in his chair and

passed a well-manicured hand over his neat grey head.

'It all seems quite clear,' he remarked. 'I must congratulate you on a neat bit of work, superintendent.'

'Once we found the tapes it was all there,' said Mr. Budd.

'It was very lucky for you they *were* found — in time,' said the assistant commissioner. 'I think, you know that it's very lucky for us that Renfrew died. It's all very clear, as I said, but it would have been difficult to convince a jury. I'm not at all sure that a clever counsel wouldn't have got him off. I wonder why Wilmot decided on such a strange form for his revenge. A play! Even if he'd got it produced, it might not have had the result that he wanted. Surely something more direct would have been better from his point of view.'

'I agree with you,' said Mr. Budd. 'But there's no doubt that he was a bit eccentric. Maybe his troubles had sent him a little off his onion, if you know what I mean?'

Colonel Blair smiled.

'Very likely you're right,' he said.

Mr. Budd got heavily to his feet.

'I'll have that report sent down, sir,' he said.

He had reached the office door when Colonel Blair said suddenly:

'What's all this I hear about Sergeant Leek?'

Mr. Budd stopped with his hand on the handle.

'About Sergeant Leek, sir?' he repeated.

'Yes. Somebody told me he's going to sing at the Wimbledon police concert. I didn't know he could sing.'

'Neither did I,' said Mr. Budd.

The assistant commissioner's eyes twinkled.

'I see,' he said.

The big man made his way slowly back to his office where he found Leek perched on his usual chair, frowning down at a notebook on his bony knee.

'Your fame is spreadin' ' said Mr. Budd. 'It's got to the ears of the A.C. now.'

The lean sergeant looked up.

'I don't know what you mean,' he said

dolefully. 'Can you think of a good rhyme for 'near'?'

'Queer,' snapped Mr. Budd.

Leek mumbled something under his breath and his long face brightened.

'That'll do,' he said, and scribbled in his notebook.

'What have you got there?' asked the stout superintendent, going over to his desk and wedging himself in his chair. 'More pop rubbish?'

'It's me new number,' explained Leek. 'You remember? I told you about it . . . '

'I remember you sayin' somethin' about bein' gaga,' broke in Mr. Budd. 'Is that it?'

The sergeant nodded.

'I'm goin' ter sing it at the concert,' he said. 'It might be taken up by a music publisher . . . '

'An' it might not,' grunted Mr. Budd. 'You're not tryin' to tell me that you're composin' the music?'

'It's the beat that matters,' said Leek.

'You'll be back on a beat, if you don't stop all this pop nonsense,' snarled his superior. 'What made you imagine you

252

could sing, anyway? You've got a voice like a crow with the croup! It's too bad even for a pop singer, an' that's sayin' somethin'.'

'You'd be surprised if I got an offer from the B.B.C.,' said the sergeant. 'This isn't a bad number. It might be all the rage. Listen . . .'

In a high-pitched voice that made the big man wince, Leek warbled:

'*I'm gaga, gaga, gaga, over you,*
'*I'm gaga, gaga, gaga, over you, baby,*
'*Whenever you are near,*
'*I come all over queer,*
'*But you're so blind you never seem to see.*
'*I'm gaga, gaga, gaga over you, baby,*
'*Couldn't you be gaga, gaga, gaga over me?*'

'There!' exclaimed Leek triumphantly. 'What d'you think of that?'

Mr. Budd glared at him. For a moment he was incapable of speech. Then he swallowed hard.

'I don't know enough suitable words to

tell you,' he snorted. 'I've heard a lot o' tripe in me time, but that . . . ' He sought vainly for a sufficiently scathing description. 'Gaga, gaga, gaga, over you! Bah!'

'It'll send 'em,' said the sergeant complacently. 'It could turn out ter be a 'golden disc' when they record it.'

'Record it!' hooted Mr. Budd derisively. 'Do you imagine that any sane company is goin' to waste good money recordin' that muck?'

Leek sighed. It was no good trying to explain to Mr. Budd. He didn't appreciate good stuff when he heard it.

'You'll see,' he said defensively. 'The teenagers 'ull go crazy over it, I'll bet.'

Mr. Budd gave him a withering look.

'The teenagers who go crazy over these pop singers are crazy anyway,' he snarled. 'You keep your mind on your job.'

Bob Hopkins came breezing into the office at that moment, the eternal Woodbine drooping from his lips.

'Hello, hello,' he greeted. 'I thought I'd just drop in to see if you were still going strong. How did you like all the nice things I said about you in the *Messenger*, eh? I did you proud, didn't I? Photograph on the front page, an' all.'

'I was beginnin' to wonder what had happened to you,' said Mr. Budd. 'Haven't seen you for nearly a week.'

'We reporters have to work for our living,' grinned Hoppy. 'We can't lounge in office chairs all the time, like the elite of Scotland Yard! I'm glad you missed me.'

'It was a good miss,' grunted Mr. Budd.

'I really popped in to see if there was anything fresh, and to give you a piece of information,' said the reporter.

'What's that?' asked the big man.

'Janice Sheridan's getting married and leaving the stage,' replied Hoppy.

'Queen Anne's dead,' retorted Mr. Budd. 'I knew that. She's marryin' that feller Crosse. I've got an invitation to the weddin'.'

'To guard the presents?' inquired Hoppy innocently. 'That's a bit of a come-down for one of the big five . . . '

'Now, look here, young feller,' said Mr. Budd sternly. 'I don't want to listen to any of your feeble jokes. I'm goin' as a guest.'

'Sorry,' apologised the unabashed Hoppy. 'Well, what about it? Is there anything in my line that's fresh?'

Mr. Budd was in the middle of shaking his head when he stopped.

'I think there is,' he said. 'You're a crime reporter, aren't you?'

Hoppy looked surprised. The big man's tone had been quite serious.

'You know I am,' he said.

'Then I've got the very job for you,' said Mr. Budd. 'Leek's singin' pop songs at the Wimbledon police concert next week. I can't think of a greater crime than that!'

'Is he?' said Hoppy with great delight. 'Is that true, sergeant?'

'Yes,' agreed Leek proudly. 'I'm goin' to sing a number of me own. Are you comin'?'

Hoppy's face expanded into one huge grin of delight.

'I wouldn't miss it for the world!' he declared.

★ ★ ★

Mr. Budd was spending a day clearing up all the 'paperwork' that had accumulated, and this was quite a considerable task. It was a job he hated, but it had to be done, and he was working at it methodically when Hoppy came in.

The stout superintendent looked up from his littered desk.

'I can't talk to you now,' he grunted. 'I'm busy. Why everythin's got to be done in triplicate, I don't know. Come in some other time . . . '

'I thought you'd like to hear about the police concert,' said Hoppy.

Mr. Budd laid down his pen.

'It was last night, wasn't it?' he said. 'Now I know why Leek hasn't come in yet. I suppose he's in hospital? What did they do? Pelt him with canteen buns?'

'You'd be surprised,' replied Hoppy. 'He was a riot! He had 'em rolling in their seats.'

Mr. Budd stared at him in astonishment.

'D'you mean to tell me that a lot of sane an' sensible policemen actually *liked* all that rubbish?' he demanded incredulously.

'Liked it?' said Hoppy. 'They howled and shouted for more.'

'I can't believe it,' declared Mr. Budd shaking his head. 'Grown men behavin' like a lot of teenagers.'

Hoppy grinned.

'They said he was the funniest thing they'd ever seen!' he answered. 'They thought he was the greatest burlesque act in the world . . . '

Mr. Budd's face changed. A light of understanding crept into his eyes.

'You mean, they didn't take him seriously?' he asked.

'Seriously!' cried Hoppy. 'You should have been there! They thought that song of his an absolute wow! The Chief Constable was laughing so much the tears were running down his face. He told me, afterwards, that Leek was the best burlesque of a pop singer he'd ever seen.'

'What's Leek think of it?' asked the stout superintendent.

'He was a bit upset, I think,' said Hoppy. 'He was quite serious about it, you see, and that made it all the funnier.'

'I hope he isn't too upset,' said Mr. Budd. 'I wouldn't like him to feel too badly about it.'

'He'll get over it,' said Hoppy. 'And he was, literally, a howling success.'

'Maybe he'll give up this pop nonsense now,' remarked Mr. Budd hopefully.

'What's going to take its place?' inquired the reporter with a grimace. 'There's sure to be something, you know.'

Mr. Budd sighed.

'That's what I'm afraid of,' he said.

THE END

Other titles in the
Linford Mystery Library:

THE DARK BOATMAN

John Glasby

Five chilling tales: a family's history is traced back for four centuries — with no instance of a death recorded . . . The tale of an aunt who wanders out to the graveyard each night . . . A manor house is built on cursed land, perpetuating the evil started there long ago . . . The fate of a doctor, investigating the ravings of a man sent mad by the things he has witnessed . . . The evil residing at Dark Point lighthouse where the Devil himself was called up . . .

CASE OF THE DIXIE GHOSTS

A. A. Glynn

America's bloody Civil War is over, leaving a legacy of bitterness, intrigues and villainy — not all acted out on the American continent. A ship from the past docks in Liverpool, England; the mysterious Mr. Fortune, carrying a burden of secrets, slips ashore and disappears into the fogs of winter. And in London, detective Septimus Dacers finds that helping an American girl in distress plunges him into combat with the Dixie Ghosts, and brings him face-to-face with threatened murder — his own.

THE LONELY SHADOWS AND OTHER STORIES

John Glasby

The midnight moon rode high and the house seemed to transmute the moonlight into something terrible. The broken chimneys stretched up like hands to the heavens, the eyeless sockets of the windows staring intently along the twisting drive. On the floor of the library, strange cabalistic designs glowed with an eerie light and there was a flickering as of corpse candles — a cold radiance, a manifestation of the evil aura which had never left this place, instead crystallising inside its very walls . . .

THE MAN OUTSIDE

Donald Stuart

Working abroad, John Fordyce and his sister returned to England after learning that John was the beneficiary of the estate of his uncle, William Grant. Taking up occupancy of Raven House, a large mansion in its own grounds, they engaged servants to run it. But soon a series of mysterious events followed. A man was seen lurking around the house, and there had been an attempted break-in. Then the chauffeur was found in the library — stabbed to death . . .

THE DEVIL'S FOOTSTEPS

John Burke

From out of the bog alongside the ancient track to the fenland village of Hexney, a line of deep footprints ran, trodden into the dry surface of the abandoned droveway. Each night, the footprints advanced nearer to the village . . . When a young boy's body was found drowned in Peddar's Lode, the villagers' ire was directed at a stranger, Bronwen Powys. The mysterious Dr. Caspian becomes her ally, but they would soon be fighting for their very lives and souls . . .

THE VENGEANCE OF LI-SIN

Nigel Vane

Jack Mallory steals a sacred idol from the temple of Tsao-Sun and brings it back to England. It contains priceless jewels, hidden by Chi   is booby-trapped pered with. Mean tries to kill Jack; Hartley, saves him heavy price for Hartley and Sir E received the same 'The vengeance of you' . . .